# Garden of the Gods

**Broken Jaw Press Inc.**
Box 596 Stn A
Fredericton NB E3B 5A6
Canada

**www.brokenjaw.com**
jblades@brokenjaw.com
tel/fax 506 454-5127

The publisher gratefully acknowledges the support of the Canada Council for the Arts and the New Brunswick Culture and Sport Secretariat-Arts Development Branch.

**National Library of Canada Cataloguing in Publication Data**

Desveaux, Dina, 1966-
    Garden of the gods / Dina Desveaux.

ISBN 1-55391-018-4

    I. Title.

PS8607.E78G37 2004        C813'.6        C2004-900304-6

# Garden of the Gods

## Dina Desveaux

Fredericton • Canada

*Dedication*

For much of time, history books have hidden the faces of women. Acadian women in North America, with the possible exception of Longfellow's *Evangeline*, have remained virtually anonymous.

I wish to dedicate this book to all the women in my life who have trusted me with their friendship and love and to the two men who inspired me to put the story on paper.

# Prologue

"Bless me Father for I do not sin very often. And, when I do, seldom tumble into that cauldron of human vices, I try to conduct myself with passionate, dare I say, religious zeal." It was 11:27 AM on the eighth of September 1984.

*Not bad for my second attempt at a confession*, I thought mockingly. Then, without thinking, I crossed myself. I was driving past the stone church in Chéticamp, an Acadian village nestled (or should I say, buried?) on the west coast of the Cape Breton Highlands. Caroline cast me a weird sideways glance. She was sitting in the passenger seat, though it was her car I was driving.

Out loud I said, "Dear Father, this is Caroline. She is my best friend and she hates to drive, but I think you should bless her too. You see, today Caroline and I are leaving Chéticamp, for good."

In those days Caroline and I shared most of our secrets, but on that day I hadn't even told her about my covert plan. I had an agenda that detailed our trip down to the last minute. The fact that we drove past the hospital (which was next to the church) sixteen years after my mother exerted that final push that propelled me into the world was no accident. I had even predicted that Caroline and my father would sit at the kitchen table that morning to share a last bowl of chocolate ice cream. In fact, sixteen years ago, a similar gust of wind had quite likely caused all the sheets and pillowcases to dance magically on the clotheslines. Back then, they were waving hello. Today they were bidding farewell.

Caroline and I had been waiting impatiently for that day. To be exact, ever since we met, when we were about four years old, we'd been griping about how BOOOORRRING Chéticamp was …

Four hours away and ten years later, I still hadn't managed to get Chéticamp out of my system. I had just passed the mid-twenties mark and my current acting gigs were barely enough to pay the bills. Denied into high society, I reinvented the Red Table Society, a fantasy world I had made up as a kid.

The game, I'll call it, all started when I was around six or seven years old. My father had some leftover paint he used on his buoys. He decided to paint an old table in the backyard and give it to me as a gift. From that day forward, although my playroom was full of toys, I began spending hours in the backyard standing at a small red table with no toys on it at all. It was there that I met you, my audience of imaginary friends.

I can't explain why exactly, but I don't like finished products. I prefer works-in-progress. Maybe it's the only way I can start anything. It doesn't have to be a final version or even a final decision, simply a work-in-progress.

I wonder how I became so obsessive. It took me almost thirty years to let go of it, perfectionism that is. Now, I've gone completely overboard. I'll try almost anything once. Only I never perfect anything. I've become what my mother would call *une bordasseuse*, a dabbler of sorts. Good God, what a useless-sounding creature … I can almost feel another confession coming on!

So when you come to visit me, you'll see all of my dabblings and other people's dabblings and mementos of the many places my dabbling lifestyle has led me. Paintings are my favourite mementos, only I hate to frame them. I mean, that would be like the end. Until it's framed, the artist can drop by for a cup coffee, grab the canvas and throw a few extra dabs of paint somewhere.

Maybe I'll make a rule. From now on, I'll only frame dead people's paintings! It's a good rule. And it seems just as reasonable as many of the rules our society lives by.

Caroline and I used to have myriad responses to what we considered stupid rules. One of our favourites was "Who made up that rule?" Another one, delivered with equal sarcasm and often addressed to Caroline's younger brother, was "Blue's green".

But getting back to our visit. In my apartment, you will also notice flowers and many books. I love flowers as long as they're not in vases. That's another thing I don't like — flowers in vases (unless of course they're in a painting). I mean, how noncreative. I think they look so much better in oversized cocktail glasses or even in one of my teapots. I collect teapots.

And why bother lining up books neatly in alphabetical order or in sections? If you came to visit me, we might spend all day searching for that one book I know is hiding somewhere. Imagine the fun we might have ...

My most generous friends say that I'm a tad eccentric. My family uses somewhat more colourful adjectives, but I won't bore you with them just yet.

I do like framing photographs. I have lots of those. Why frame photographs and not paintings? Simple. Photographs are a done deal. You can't change the past. May as well forget about it, I say.

It's all just spare change. I'd probably be better off throwing the nickels and dimes to the homeless instead of fountains. Someone should be making wishes for them. I should just move on, never look back ... if only I could stop being so damn sentimental. Like brooding over that picture hanging above my mantel. Take a look:

"Isabelle, where are you going?" Caroline demands. I can't answer her, so I give her my *I'm-the-one-driving* look. It's the same look my father used to give my mother and one of the few things in life I have perfected.

"Here we are," I announce as dispassionately as possible for a teenager leaving home forever. I climb out of the car with my camera and start setting it up on the hood with the self-timer. I grab Caroline's arm. We scramble over towards the edge of the water. As the shutter clicks, we both spontaneously lift our hands and make that universally-recognized symbol. Some think of it as peace whereas others regard it as a symbol of victory.

The photograph stands the test of irony in that it was only on the day I left Chéticamp for good that I was finally capable of seeing how perfectly enchanting the place was. Behind us, the church towered above the colourful wooden houses of the village. The rooftops and the softly billowing sheets created a human landmark kissing both the ocean coastline and the mountains of the highlands.

For a moment as I stood gazing wistfully, I thought I saw a familiar face waving at me from across the harbour. She seemed real until I noted that she was floating above the sheets. I blinked and she was gone, leaving a whisper in the wind that I couldn't make out. Also gone was the beauty and softness I had glimpsed. In its place was a hardness, the edge of a blade that made me shudder as I turned my back on this small village in a small time. Stubbornness kept me from turning. I walked on ignoring the clouds of butterflies floating on a breeze that purred like a cat and tried to hug me. It was no use. My skin had turned too hard to notice.

On a final note to the people who regarded us as sarcastic teenage brats, I will add one final confession. When we got into the car that day we left Chéticamp forever, there were only two people, Caroline and myself, who felt instinctively that this community had let us down. There is an African proverb that says it takes a village to raise a child. However, a lesser-known quote, about another small community, states: "Many of my oppressors enjoyed the blessing of poverty, but it did not seem to do very much to improve their so-called moral character."

We got back into the car and neither Caroline nor I stopped crying until we were long past the Canso Causeway.

*(Blackout)*

# Act One
*Mise-en-scène*

*Props*: A frame, some canvas, wool and ... a hooker!

Chéticamp — August 25, 2000

*Bonjour*, Terry!

8:53 sharp: The sun just leapt out from behind the Highlands. After two consecutive days of drizzle and grey skies, the contrast is surreal. The way the white light teases the brilliant blue sky reminds me of a French dance move called *chassé-croisé*. Today, the dance partners are tree tops and infinity. Oh, look, all the birds of the forest have decided to join in the dance and add their beautiful sonatas. Crisp air, vivid colours — life is indeed beautiful. Best of all, in one week I am going back to Halifax!

Terry, you'll never guess what I found last night! It was very late & I decided to start packing. While looking for boxes in the attic, I discovered the most intriguing treasure! A hooked rug of a woman. A NUDE, BLACK WOMAN! Since the most common motif in Chéticamp hooked rugs is flowers (and not the Georgia O'Keefe kind either), this rug is one-of-a-kind! It was rolled up in a carton with my name on it! (Technically it could be my grandmother's name, since she and I share the same name) Must ask Mama after work where it came from and who it belongs to? *Très bizarre!*

I don't know whether you will read this email before you leave for Brittany, but I thought of a sound you should listen for if you happen to be by the ocean during your vacation:

Find a spot where waves are rushing up to a pebbled beach and listen carefully for the music of the ocean as it rises to a crescendo. When the ocean has you captivated as its audience, you can hear the applause as the waves retreat over the pebbles. It's a strange paradox, Terry. When I grew up in Chéticamp and listened to that applause, I used to imagine being all grown up and attending the symphony or the opera. Now whenever I hear applause at the symphony, all I can think about is the sound of the ocean.

My second recommendation for your holiday is *Le Petit Prince*. I'll admit I read mostly in English now (a childish rebellion against my cultural roots that sadly became a habit). Nevertheless, even as a *grande personne*, I try to carry *Le Petit Prince*'s ideology in my heart.

I am still worried that you might turn out to be an online axe murderer. You haven't even answered my questions so I will answer only two of yours. Someone once described me as mentally flamboyant. Secondly, I have no idea what ISO refers to. Icky Sticky Organism was the first thing to come to mind, but I've probably been reading too much about fungus, algae and lichen lately!

Anyway, hope you have a great vacation. Cheers!

Your Acadian friend, Isabelle

PS      No word on Paris job — bleak …

Paris — August 31, 2000

*Chère* Isabelle,

Are you still in Chéticamp? About the whole axe murderer thing. Rest assured I've not butchered a single person and they never did get that assault thing to stick :) So you see, you have nothing to fear. Unless, of course, I'm lying. If I were an axe murder, chances are I might conceal that information during just these types of correspondences. I guess you'll have to take a leap of faith. In the meantime, I can send you my mug shot — oops, I mean photo!

I like how you described yourself — mentally flamboyant. I'd like to think we're alike in that respect, though I don't feel quite as bold in my proclamation. Isabelle, I love how you described the sound of the ocean. So I found a pebbled beach during my holiday and listened for the applause — you were right. I also felt the queerest sensation as though you were there with me. Also on your advice, I took *Le Petit Prince* with me on my excursion in Brittany. It was delightful.

Here are a few answers. Besides being immersed in academia, I love painting, hiking and going to the theatre. Good wine, my dog Chocolat, and gypsy music are my favourite companions. Oh, yeah, when I lived in Québec our family had a cottage by the lake where we enjoyed many nights of board games. I'll warn you though, I have a competitive streak!

I have come up with a list of new questions:
    Favourite food? Favourite colour? Favourite animal? Wildest dreams?
    Who would you invite to dinner (ANY six people)?
    How do you feel about being an Acadian?
    What is ultimate reality?
    Where did I put my new sunglasses?
    What's the scoop on that hooked rug?

By the way, how are things with you & Tony? Will he still be in the apartment when you go back?

I confess I don't know much about Acadians or hooked rugs. This is an aspect of French culture that I'd like to learn more about before I move to Nova Scotia. For starters, you could share your experience of growing up as an Acadian, *non*?

It's getting late. Just started to rain again — one aspect of Paris I'm still not used to. My painting studio/bedroom is in the loft, so I hear the spattering quite clearly. I do like the sound.

Your pen pal,
Terry

PS    Any word on the job in Paris yet? I'm still checking into apartments for you, but they're about as scarce as hen's teeth.

# Chapter 1
## Halifax: Dead Heat

On September 28, 2000, Halifax was encroached by a late season scorcher. The ocean breeze that usually rustled the skirts of Nova Scotia's capital (unlike the wild squalls that conspired to rid Chéticamp of its clotheslines) was gone. In its stead, stood a canvas of thirsty trees. Still life.

Just on the edge of the canvas where the peninsula dropped into a stagnant Halifax Harbour was the historic harbourfront and just beyond it, the small downtown district, highlighted by Spring Garden Road. This was my new home, a road where spring and new beginnings were always possible. I picked a flat with obvious fortitude, one of the few places that had survived the Halifax Explosion. This, I felt gave it character.

That day will also remain etched in the memory of many Canadians because it marked the death of our most charismatic leader to date, Pierre Elliot Trudeau.

On the Tuesday following Trudeau's death, I was one of millions glued to the television screen as his son Justin delivered the most eloquent eulogy I had ever heard. Even my roommate Tony, who usually despised all affairs even remotely related to politics, became engrossed in the sad affair ...

When the funeral coverage ended, Tony got up and shut the television off. We did everything to avoid looking at each other. While he was banging at the piano keys, I stared at my mysterious hooked rug.

Although the reclining nude faced away from the artist and seemed to suggest a separation between the artist and the model, there was a lingering intimacy in the work. If the artist had been peering in on the naked woman, the work nonetheless communicated a sensual knowledge of the model more typical of a lover. The subtle variations in the shades of wool must have taken endless hours to perfect. I knew about this arduous task from years of observing my parents and grandparents dying their own wool.

When I looked at it more closely, I noticed that it had a quality reminiscent of a charcoal drawing, which might explain why the woman's skin seemed so dark. It was possible that the shadowy figure had white skin that just seemed darker because of the low light. This made more sense since to my recollection there were no African Canadians living in Chéticamp when I grew up. What did stand out was how the artist seemed to have caressed the canvas to smooth the harsh lines of the model, touching her body and soul in ways that not many humans know.

Tony had stopped playing. The combination of silence and heat in the apartment was about to drive me stark raving batty. I grabbed my red Italian sunglasses to camouflage the red puffiness around my eyes, checked my mourning attire and headed down the stairs.

From the bottom landing, I called out, "Tony, I'm off to the coffee shop. Catch you later."

"Sorry, I can't join you. I'm meeting up with Calum later and won't be back for supper." In other words, Tony was pissed off that I hadn't asked him to join me. It was his sarcastic way of communicating just that. "I'll also be needing my jacket."

I didn't want to deal with Tony today. And how did he know I was wearing his leather jacket? All I wanted was to buy a newspaper and pore over the articles relating to Trudeau's life and death.

Five minutes later I stood in front of a coffee shop retrieving a newspaper from one of those dispensing boxes on the street. I hesitated before closing its door. There was only one other paper left. I considered taking it, thinking that it might be handy to have an extra copy for teaching purposes. Cowardice won out in the end. I couldn't risk the possible embarrassment of having someone see me take two newspapers for the price of one. I headed into the café, with one, single copy tucked under my arm.

Even a month after returning from Chéticamp, I still felt a wave of sheer delight at the prospect of sitting, anonymous, unique, and completely at ease in one of the many Spring Garden Road cafés.

Halifax came alive in September when all the university students arrived. Meanwhile, fall in Chéticamp always reminded me of the beginning of a slow and painful death. Back home, there was a good expression used to describe someone who took too much time and held you up; they were like *la mort après le plaint*. After the last long weekend in October, Chéticamp definitely reminded me of death after a moan.

This was also the time of year when my folks used to take out the frame at which they would spend countless hours hooking rugs for the next tourist season. I always relished telling strangers that my parents were part-time "hookers".

The café was nearly empty, since the usual office break was over and the lunch crowd hadn't arrived yet. The tables were round and crammed into as little space as possible. As usual, I sat at a window seat so I could feel the sunshine on my face. The open window served to lessen my guilt about smoking in public even if this was one rare place that still permitted smokers to sin.

Considering that I look back on this day as a kind of celestial freak show when all the stars aligned to cause a cosmic portal where past and present came together, it began unremarkably. Aside from Trudeau's death and the heat that refused to release its stranglehold on Halifax, everything else appeared normal.

I did notice that my neighbour Cliff wasn't at his regular table. Instead, he sat at the one by the door. He was glaring at the two older men sitting at the table behind mine. On my way back from the counter, I recognized the one facing me as a recent newcomer to the growing number of homeless on Spring Garden. My initial curiosity was mostly due, however, to a little game I always liked playing: identifying French accents. Although my back was to them, I leaned back to eavesdrop.

*"Ouain, Ouain, les enfants d'aujourd'hui."*

It was Québécois for sure and not Acadian. Ah, it was Montréal, the same accent as Tony's. Too easy. With the matter resolved, I lost interest.

Instead of reading the paper as I had intended, I just stared at Pierre Trudeau's picture. Those two men from Québec probably wouldn't have understood my grief. They probably felt like many of the separatists who despised Trudeau's nationalistic style of politics.

My pen pal Terry went so far as to confess resentment not just towards Trudeau but towards Acadians, due to their misplaced patriotism. Being a separatist, Terry felt that most Acadians were spineless in the fight to preserve cultural rights (though she seemed to suspend her disapproval in my case). Apparently, Terry didn't understand the concept of oppression unless it was accompanied with a certain revolutionary spirit. Then again, Terry had moved to Paris. So much for her dauntless spirit of revolution.

Trudeau had been my childhood hero. When I was seven, my parents took me to 24 Sussex Drive so that I could see where he lived. Mam and Pape even adopted the lessons that Pierre taught his kids and strived to teach me in a similar fashion. Growing up, I heard all the reasons why I should believe in myself, treat others with respect and develop the skills and sensibilities to become an exemplary citizen.

*"Peux-tu croire? Cette p'tite estécrabe avait cassé la windshield de mon char flambant neuf?"*

That matter-of-fact question coming from the table behind mine caught my attention, since I too had once broken the windshield of a neighbour's car. That meant that somewhere out there was an enfant terrible with as much spit and vinegar as I had. I wondered if the child was also carrying around the burden of guilt of having ruined someone else's life in the process?

I probably never would have travelled as much were it not for Pierre Trudeau. But, Pierre believed in travelling the world in order to gain first-hand cultural experience, so my parents invested much of their life savings in order that I might follow those same ideals. Pierre also believed in higher education, and so, come hell or high water, I was going be the first in the family to graduate from university.

Years later, it wouldn't be my perseverance that Dad would mention when I landed a government job. "Don't forget that none of this would have been possible if it hadn't been for Trudeau's efforts in securing bilingualism in Canada." It was okay, though, because I knew that to his friends he boasted of my brilliance. Boasting was one of my father's tragic flaws. We all have those. Mine seemed to involve men.

Wait a second. That man with the unmistakable Québécois accent had used the word *estécrabe*, which was an Acadian expression. I squinted to try to detect any vestiges of the guttural Acadian phonetics lurking beneath the nasal punctuation of his Québécois slang. Have you ever seen people do that before? It's inconsequential since squinting has nothing to do with listening.

Squinting reminded me of Louis, a old co-worker from a restaurant I'd worked at during high school. Louis used to squint often in his efforts to eavesdrop on conversations. He also developed an entire new language to animate his discoveries.

Louis referred to the Québécois' unique way of speaking as a bunch of chickens clucking. He said they had an extensive range of high and low notes, with random emphasis on certain syllables. Assuming Louis was right, I had to conclude that this man behind me sounded more like a clucking chicken than any other animal I could think of. I almost laughed out loud, but turned instead to check on my neighbour.

Cliff was still glaring, but now his beady eyes were focused in my direction. I just rolled my eyes nonchalantly, took a long drag on my cigarette and blew the smoke in his direction. Suzette, who worked behind the counter, noticed this little exchange and chuckled.

*"Un autre café, Joe?"*

No, this time it wasn't the accent, but the voice that made me pause. I was about to turn around and ask where he was from, when his companion jumped to his feet, bolted past Cliff and ran outside.

I watched him racing towards the same box where I had bought my paper. A man in his forties dressed in an expensively cut suit, an Armani I noted, had just inserted his coins into the box. He opened the door with one hand and was about to reach in with the other when, the older man pushed him aside, grabbed the door, snatched the last newspaper and ran back inside.

The Armani suit caught my eye and gaped at me as if daring me to answer a question. I was thinking that he seemed familiar somehow, but my lack of reaction must have annoyed him. He shifted his restless eyes to chase the Spring Garden Road traffic. Perhaps he was hoping for a stranger's sympathy. Finding none, he threw his hands up in the air and stormed off.

Just then, Tony roared by on his Harley. He was wearing his leather jacket and didn't even glance towards the café.

I turned around just in time to catch the homeless man giving the newspaper to Suzette. How positively bizarre was that? The entire scene was utterly surreal. Had I known how desperate he was for a newspaper, I could have given him my copy. Or better yet, when I'd had the opportunity, I could have taken both copies, given him one and kept the other. But, he hadn't even wanted it for himself. Could he read even? He hadn't given the newspaper a second glance, but had given it away to Suzette, who was now leaning on the counter casually flipping through the damn thing.

It occurred to me that the same man had been sitting there when I had opened the box but hadn't tried to steal my paper. Why was that? Had he seen me? Was it because I was a woman? Or could it be that this was some weird game in which the object was to obtain the last newspaper in the box? None of the possibilities I conjured made any sense.

I refocused my attention in time to overhear the newspaper thief thanking his companion for breakfast. He added that he had better make himself scarce in case the "suit" decided to send the cops after him.

As soon as the door had closed behind him, I turned around and tapped his companion on the shoulder.

"Excuse me but you wouldn't be from Chéticamp by any ..."

Before the last word was out, he had interrupted me.

"Isabelle, is that you? Holy shit, I haven't laid eyes on you for what ... it must be twenty years? Come over here and sit with me." He motioned to the seat previously occupied by the newspaper thief.

As I got up with coffee and newspaper in hand, I knew I was about to move up a notch on Cliff's shit list. Now, I was moving to his table.

"Gilles, long time no see. How've you been?"

"Bella, Bella, Bella, look at you all grown up and beautiful as ever. You know you haven't changed one bit. I bet if you were wearing pigtails, you'd look exactly the same. I can hardly believe I was just talking about you."

"Hey, I heard your dad passed away. So sad. Such a nice man. He paid for the windshield, you know. Took time off from work, put a plastic sheet on the window and drove the car to Sydney himself to replace it. He was always a gentleman, that one. But you, what about you, what have you been up to?"

He paused for breath. I knew I had better say something quickly or he might never let me get a word in. Suddenly, I remembered why he had annoyed me so much even at the tender age of four.

"Oh, this and that." I told him about graduating from university in the spring and spending the summer working in Chéticamp, but I couldn't tell whether or not he had heard anything I'd said. He continued his breathless recital.

"What about your mother, is she still living? I heard she had cancer awhile back. You know I've only been back to Chéticamp once in the last twenty years and that was for Mom's funeral. Thank God, Dad has moved in with my sister. Remember Adilia? She's a doctor now. Did you know that? Anyway, I don't have to worry that he'll be waked in that godawful hellhole. Sorry, I shouldn't say that. You probably don't hate the place like me. You didn't grow up in a family poor like mine though. Bastards. Not your family though … your parents were the kindest souls. Boy, did we luck out. You know what else your father did? He bought me oils, and every now and then, he would arrive from having worked away with a canvas for me. He knew my folks couldn't afford 'em. He encouraged me to become an artist. Said he'd never had the guts to do it himself. But, he had talent too. I remember his hooked rugs, especially the ones with stormy seas. He really loved the ocean, used to give me tips on how to improve mine …"

As I first listened to Gilles speaking, I noticed the absence of "th"s in his speech. "This" became "dis" and "that" became "dat". I used to speak like him once. Then I noticed his hands, raw and severely blistered, but tried not to stare at them. How painful it must have been to paint with those sores. I wanted to ask if he'd been burned, but refrained from doing so in case he painted me a typical, meddlesome Cheticamper.

"Gilles, I still remember the first painting of yours I saw. It was a small pastel of a single sunflower. I thought it was the most beautiful thing I'd ever seen. Are you still painting?" I had a class to teach in less than two hours and this was probably not the best question to ask if I wanted to get out of there any time soon.

For the next few minutes Gilles embarked on another enthusiastic spiel about his success as a visual artist in Montreal. I felt overcome with sadness at his lack of social grace. I truly understood how that could have resulted from his childhood. An alcoholic father and daily rows between the parents. Had it not been for unusual circumstances, I might've turned out just like him, awkward, fidgety and bordering on the neurotic. A more disturbing idea was that I might be more like him than I cared to admit. Though since I had named Neurotica, I found it easier to order her around. At his next pause, I told Gilles that I had to go because I was teaching a class at Dalhousie.

Gilles began to laugh loudly. "Dal! You mean the university. Here I am yammering away about my life and you are teaching at Dalhousie!"

I told him it wasn't that glamorous. I was filling in for a month or so teaching one class. Otherwise, I was unemployed and looking for full-time work. "But not to worry, Gilles, I'm not considering a life of crime just yet."

"The good thing about this is that you have time to get together with me for coffee again soon? It'll be my treat. It's the least I can do to repay your father for how much he encouraged my career." He was scribbling his name and number on a piece of paper. I reciprocated by giving him mine.

"I hope you'll call me soon. Hey, wait a minute. Can I have your address too, just in case?"

I hesitated but decided there could be no harm in giving it to him. As I wrote it down, my natural curiosity got the best of me.

"That man who was here with you earlier, why on earth did he steal a newspaper and then give it away?"

"Oh, that, yeah … well, Joe is a nice homeless fellow I take out for breakfast sometimes, 'cause like I said, I remember what it's like to be poor. Anyway, he always insists on paying the tip. Today, he decided that a good tip would be a newspaper."

"Any idea why he didn't steal it from me?"

"No. My guess is you didn't look rich enough. You look more bohemian. In fact, if someone walked in and was guessing which one of us is the artist, I bet they would pick you every time. But Joe, no, he'd never steal from anyone who wasn't rich."

"Oh." I got up and started to fold up my newspaper when an idea occurred to me.

"Gilles, before I dash off, you wouldn't by any chance know who the most artistic hookers in Chéticamp were or anybody in particular who might have been hooking nudes during the time you lived there?"

"Nudes? You've got to be kidding. The only hooked rugs I remember were so lame they could have been auctioned off at a church fundraiser … Why d'you ask?"

"What about African Canadians. Do you know if anyone dark-skinned lived in Chéticamp?"

"Now you're really out on a branch. Aside from being all white, everyone was French and Catholic except a few English families who had businesses in the area. But that was only because of the back-stabbing going on between the French who dared to set up a business."

I wasn't entirely in agreement. After all, the co-operative movement had very strong roots in Chéticamp and sharing wealth was a very worthwhile socialist principle. Out loud I said, "You're forgetting the Jehovah's Witnesses. They also lived in Chéticamp. And now there's even an established Buddhist community."

"Oh, yeah. They segregated too?"

I really did have to run. I said that when we got together for coffee I would tell him more about my rug.

"For whatever it's worth, there is one woman from Chéticamp who's done some recent abstracts with hooked rugs. Her name is Yvette, but I think she's living somewhere in Europe. Your sister Judith might know. I think they were good friends in high school."

I'd been meaning to call Judith anyway. Now I had an excuse. I hesitated before giving Gilles a hug. It felt like hugging a store mannequin. He returned about as much physical responsiveness. Yet his eyes were as warm as a puppy dog gazing at a sunny sky.

As I left the coffee shop, I thought about how weird the morning had been. I had run into an old neighbour whose windshield I had smashed in revenge when I was a kid, had witnessed a modern day Robin Hood type in action, and watched an Armani suit lose its cool.

What would my family think of my city life if they were here? With no Armani suits or coffee shops to distract them, they were undoubtedly immersed in the mourning of Pierre. If I were there, we would be mourning together.

•    •    •

Six hours later, I was running up the stairs to try to catch the telephone before the answering machine picked up. I tripped over one of Tony's shirts and cursed. The machine picked up. It was Francesca. "Hey, Isabelle, it's me. You'll never guess what happened when I was out at a coffee shop today? I'm at Tom's, meeting with the school staff. Why don't you drop by and I'll tell you all about it."

My first instinct was to glance out the window to check whether the moon was full …

# Chapter 2
## Every Dog Returns to His Vomit

Okay, I'll admit it. When Caroline and I sped away from Cape Breton all those years ago, nobody (including me) would have dreamed that either of us would ever go back to live there, even temporarily. But in September of 1989 a series of events began to unfold, leading to that very decision. It all started after I met John, my first true love.

We came into a clearing outside the cover of tall buildings. The orange moon loomed above, seemingly buoyant in the mist.

"How perfectly round", he said. "Nature is sending us a message."

"Of what?"

"Perfection — that it will never be denied. It is always within our grasp to live in a perfect world."

"Then you do believe in all that stuff?" I interjected.

"What stuff?"

"You know. The magic, the fortune teller, and the invisible dancing bear." We were turning the corner that led to the bar where we'd first discovered we were in love.

"All right," he laughed. "But just for tonight." He looked into my eyes. He said they were round and perfect, but that they had lost the look of the schoolgirl. When he looked into them he claimed that he could see something no one else saw. When I pestered him for an explanation, he said it was a reflection of dark mysterious thoughts hiding behind two soft blue moons.

"John, what do you want most right at this moment?" We were perched on barstools. His hand was caressing my thigh.

"What I desperately want is for all the lights to go out, I want everybody in the room to disappear and I want to kiss you like you've never been kissed before."

"Then let's get out of here!"

For the rest of that night, I put aside all irrational fears about three tarot cards that had appeared in my reading earlier that day. Around the time the moon was about to give way to the sun, Dvořák's "Song to the Moon" made the earth tremble and reconsider sunrise. I lay in his arms, spent, unaware that the trinity of doom, the Three, Nine and Ten of Swords, were poised for a swift sharp assault on my current state of rapture. Looking back, I can also see why I became so obsessed with perfection.

My love,

The dusk lengthens. I see you, silent, clear, in the iridescence of winter. You are a moment that pivots my disconcerted spirit.

We are constantly reaching for one another in books, in letters and in crystal balls. With the moon as my witness, I promise you this:

We are forever united in the vast nothingness that is the blue sky filled with clouds that reveal invisible dancing bears to us; and in the night sky as boundless as our love.

But we will fall to earth and be together again here soon.

Yours forever,
Isabelle

I was right about one thing. We fell.

The events that conspired to bring me back to Chéticamp really descended a few short months after I sent that last letter. Years later, I would imagine the trees in Point Pleasant Park falling in similar domino fashion during Hurricane Juan.

When John got back I was *folle comme un balai* as they say in Chéticamp. I guess I lost it when my sister called to say my father's cancer had spread to his liver. He would be coming to Halifax by ambulance in the morning.

The morning came, but the ambulance never showed up. My father had died in Chéticamp. It was probably for the best. He hated the city.

As I sank into deep depression my relationship with John began its own slow demise. Three weeks following the funeral, I had a miscarriage. Those were some of the final tender moments that John and I shared.

A little over a year after my father died, I buried my relationship with John alongside Dad's grave, only to exhume both bodies, to attend yet another funeral. This time it was my thirty-year-old brother, killed in a horrific fire.

This loss seemed the most unbearable. The last afternoon I had spent with Jean-Claude ended on a sour note. For years his racist comments had been driving me crazy. I had finally gotten up the courage to talk to him about it. As we shared our last cup of tea together, which he always insisted on drinking in fine bone china, he made an unsavoury comments about the Chinese who were about to take over the world. I reacted by accidentally dropping my teacup on the floor.

"You should have more respect for china."

"Yeah, well, so should you." Those five words still haunt me today. I can still imagine the rest of his teacups exploding one by one in the fire that stole Jean-Claude from my family. And although I know it's illogical, I somehow feel that in breaking the first tea cup I was responsible for starting that ugly chain of explosions.

I began avoiding all criticism in personal relationships. It was easy. When someone I loved said or did anything to upset me, I would simply change the subject. Never again would someone I loved die with any bad words unresolved.

I was *en pantène*, a prolonged agony. The joy and wonder that I had found since coming to Halifax were killed off like a garden of annuals after an unmerciful frost. If there were any perennials in that garden waiting to emerge, they were impossible to detect during that interminable icy winter. Even I knew that every garden had perennials. I called them weeds.

I quit my job and went backpacking in Europe. Eventually, I settled in Spain. And instead of finding consolation for my aching soul I lost myself in books and architecture. Then, one day, I received a fat envelope in the mail from John. It was a love story about two Acadians I knew well, my parents.

Not long after that, I packed my bags and returned to Halifax. It was also due in part to John's short story that I began toying with the idea of researching my Acadian heritage. My father would have liked that. So, I started making plans that would allow me to go back. Too much time had elapsed. Besides, I had unfinished business to settle in Chéticamp ...

I knew that trying to write a novel was a hideous idea. I didn't have a writer's ability to see beyond myself. On many occasions I was tempted to explain this to my downstairs neighbour Cliff who was stuck in his own existential predicament, trying to write the most serious novel of the century. Perhaps if I'd told him about my work-in-progress theory, he would have stopped scowling all the time and chilled out. He was making it next to impossible for me to pretend that all was hunky-dory in the world.

Where was I? Oh, right, going back to Chéticamp. So, I orchestrated my return by enrolling in a Bachelor of Education degree, leaving my summers open to work in my hometown. In some ambiguous, unpredictable and synchronous manner such as life presents us with at times, my old high school friend Caroline was infected with the same idea. Fifteen years after we had graduated from high school, Caroline and I found ourselves in the same classes again.

We had always kept in touch, but our lives had taken two completely different paths. After losing Papape, who had given so much meaning to my youth, and losing John, who had given meaning to my twenties, I reinvented my life to ensure that it was bustling with meaningful activity.

At the same rate as my emptiness grew, so did my daytime planner. Whether it was social justice activism, community volunteering, or my traffic jam of a social life, I was always consumed by something. Meanwhile, Caroline quietly went about her way, leading a more reclusive life as many an academic does. Her decision to become a public school teacher was a complete mystery to me.

When I first broached the subject to Caroline about going to Chéticamp to work for the summer, disbelief was written all over her face. She had that look one has when they're about to admit a family member into an asylum.

It was the first hot spring day. We had spent most of it at Point Pleasant Park. We'd brought along a radio, some suntan lotion and an essay that was due for the next day's class. In addition to the essay, we were also expected to bring an object to represent something about our school years. I was bringing a colourful tropical fish candle that Caroline had given me. I thought it was an appropriate metaphor for my high school days: A fish out of water, with a colourful façade but an unlit wick.

For the first time we discussed what had happened to us back then. We had known each other for nearly thirty years, but had to wait twenty of them before we could discuss something so critical. Was it a bond we shared or was it more like bondage?

Once again, I began battling the demons of my guilty conscience. I was having recurring nightmares about Père Chiasson, the local priest, in a wheelchair because of my stupidity. Every night he found new and devious ways to get back at me. Fortunately, I had urgent packing to consume me during the day.

A few weeks later, there I was, driving east over Halifax's MacDonald Bridge in a rental van packed with the basics I would need to furnish the old homestead. I also had some not-so-basics, such as my paintings, as well as two dozen flower pots, potting soil and seedlings just beginning to poke their shiny green leaves up out of the soil. I was going to plant my very first garden!

I figured I might need a therapeutic pastime if I was going to confront this unfinished business in Chéticamp. Secrecy, silence and shame. Those were the pillars of oppression I remembered. The only rivals were gossip, opinionated loudmouths and pride.

At least that's how I felt before going back there.

How could I have known that a discovery in my hometown and a new pen pal were about to send me on an adventure to a faraway land and time that would change everything I had believed thus far to be true?

Out loud I said, *"Mémére Bella et Papape, aidez-moi."*

*Bella and her son, P'tit Pierre, who had been startled to hear the sound of their names, looked at one another.*

*— Poor Isabelle, said P'tit Pierre. I guess she'll never know the whole truth behind that accident.*

*— Even you don't know the whole truth, my son, said Bella.*

*— What do you mean, I don't know the whole truth, Mother?*

*— Don't you think it would be more fun if I showed you?*

*— Mother, you're not thinking of sending Isabelle to the attic, are you?*

*— Just watch, my son.*

## Chapter 3
### Learning to Love Seagulls

The surprise came when I found myself in a community of cheerful people who, for the most part, appeared disinterested in my affairs and gave me no reason to dislike them. Still, I couldn't let go of the suspicion that they were protecting themselves with a veneer of *bonhomie*.

I had become one of them. It was as if we, like our ancestors before us, were on guard. To make matters worse, I wasn't just assimilated, I was returning from the prime assimilating city, the very city where Governor Charles Lawrence had ordered the Deportation of the Acadians. As for me, I was armed with my city ways and that, in Chéticamp, is as repulsive. Can't say that I blame them, either.

I remember my initial disbelief to these city ways. I had arrived in Halifax elated and eager to explore my new home. What better way than to go for a stroll downtown.

"Hello! How are you today?" I said to the first person I saw. My greeting was met with a blank stare.

"Hi, nice day isn't it?" This was met with a squint that said *do I know you?* Later, when one of my greetings was met with a scowl that bordered on rage I adjusted. I kept smiling at people and discovered that even city folks will smile back.

In the end, I also decided that the brushstroke I'd painted my childhood community with had been unfairly wide and generalized. Besides, I could never forget the support of countless parishioners during my family's time of crisis.

As in any small town, there were exceptions, a few eccentrics and nonconformists. Some of these individuals resurfaced in my memory when I found myself in the old house all alone. All I could figure was that the bitter squalls of my teenage angst had obliterated the sweeter impact of these exceptional, if short-lived acquaintances.

One thing that had remained consistent in Chéticamp was the level of boredom which lifted as quickly as a fast-moving fogbank at the first hint of summer, which also coincided with my four-month stint there. In Chéticamp, nearly everyone suffered from boredom at one time or another, and when this occurred, they (like me when I lived there) devoted themselves to the cultivation of habits.

Some of the most common habits were drinking excessively, playing bingo or cards, and developing a roving eye for the neighbour's spouse. Maybe The Ten Commandments hadn't been properly explained at the local church. Albeit, some of the more oppressed women who did get the message found salvation in obsessive-compulsive housecleaning. Meanwhile, there were men who did the same with work outside the home, but this seemed to be done more for profit than for salvation.

The habit I disliked most was *parler des autres*. These busybodies reminded me of seagulls scavenging for their next meal. They could strip even the most respectable person into piecemeal. The only recourse for this assault was patience. Like the wind, it would change directions and targets given time.

About two months into my stay in Chéticamp, I bought a carved seagull from a local folk artist. It's not perfect, but who needs perfection when life is afoot?

On a livelier note, music was a common ingredient that kept even the most cabin-fevered and desperate of cases from complete insanity, lifting them into stints of jubilation. Now, there was something I could relate to. I loved gypsy music. It was while I was listening to an old Django Reinhardt remix that a thought occurred to me.

Just as the gypsies had done, Acadians had absorbed the language and the music of the surrounding culture yet had managed to transform it into something beautiful, real and enduring.

We survived despite prejudice. We survived the Deportation. But could we continue surviving if no one ever talked about or wrote about the denial?

I had become a city girl, but this had in no way erased my fear that saying it out loud might make things worse. The silence was so loud sometimes that when I listened carefully I could still hear its echo in the conversations of the many Acadians who tried to avoid the claws of history. They were hard to spot. They had so politely allowed themselves to be assimilated that they were virtually undetectable.

I should know. I was one of them.

Gypsies and Acadians, exiled, scorned and later romanticized. As the summer wore on in Chéticamp, I had to acknowledge that I loved gypsy music so much because I was mourning my own cultural loss and displacement.

Once I had that one figured out, it was much easier to do as everyone else did. I started listening to Celtic music and even attended barn dances. The only thing I haven't done yet is participate in a square dance, though I'm certain it's bound to happen sooner or later. Remember, I'll try anything once …

A traditional Cape Breton square dance. "Do-si-do and promenade". Somewhere a caller's voice from the past reminded me that these were French expressions. *Quelle ironie!*

I was also curious about how the latest batch of youth living in Chéticamp were making out. But, as with everything else, I didn't find anything highly unusual. My summer job in eco-tourism included giving guided hikes to local students and chaperoning school groups on outdoor expeditions such as windsurfing, canoeing and kayaking. Imagine me — an adult chaperon!

With the exception of being curiously drawn to two girls in one of the groups and finding out later, in typical Cape Breton fashion, that they were my second cousins, I didn't observe anything that would've distinguished these teens from any of the ones I worked with in Halifax. They spoke a different language and manifested some undeniably rural mannerisms, but that was about it.

So I discarded my notion about researching or even writing about Acadians. I couldn't think of anything to write about. The only hen scratching I did that whole summer was to my French pen pal

Terry, who was helping me scour for an apartment in Paris in case I got lucky and landed the dream job I'd applied for.

First, though, I had a puzzle to solve. I was off to Halifax with a mysterious hooked rug. Little did I know that the yarns of a far more compelling and interwoven tale were about to start unravelling before my very eyes. It was a tale at least as compelling as the one of my childhood gripes. Be forewarned, though, there could be some griping along the way. I wouldn't be from Cape Breton unless I griped once in awhile … with good reason, of course!

Halifax, September 4th

*Chère* Terry

I was almost out the door when the dreaded phone call came. No job in Paris for me! I sort of suspected the worst when so much time had elapsed. Still it's a blow. I guess I should be grateful that they had the decency to call me in person rather than send one of those godawful form letters.

Unlike the first time I left some fifteen years ago, this departure is less frantic and more sentimental. I will miss some of life's simplest pleasures, like watching my neighbour Priscille as she goes about attending to her family with the same magic my mother used to. Almost every day she puts out clothes to dry. She has made an art of it. I love to sit and watch her lovely colour-coordinated sheets, pillowcases and towels dance in the ocean breeze. Sometimes I imagine I'm inside the pillowcases, floating. Other days, when brightly-coloured children's clothing adorn the line, I get to dance inside them in wild abandon.

As I'd expected, saying goodbye to my mother was hardest of all. I think all humans must be half-caterpillar and half-butterfly. Mama was like a butterfly all summer, but today I could feel her beginning a slow retreat into her cocoon, and it's my fault. What kind of a horrible creature am I to nurture the caterpillar when I possess the vigour to give her wings?

Thank God, I have my hooked rug to distract me. I was thinking that if you were interested, I could mail you a book about hooked rugs, but I'd need your non-virtual address for that. I keep wondering how old it is. It makes me think of history and whether or not we are bound to repeat it. What do you think?

Terry, have you ever been part of An Evening of Murder? I refer here to a game and not your seedy criminal past (I have overcome my axe murderer theory). I ask for two reasons. First, they're a blast and if you haven't, you should try it. Maybe I'll tempt you into coming to Halifax by inviting you to one. Could be an interesting way to meet ...

Besides, I think that murdering with an axe is probably more of a male thing. One thing I will never do is respond to personal ads in order to meet men. They are not exactly high on my trust list these days. More about that later …

Isabelle

Paris, September 5th

Chère Isabelle,

An Evening of Murder? I must be doing better than I thought. From potential axe murderer to … potential axe murderer. Hey, wait a second!

I have the perfect setting for an evening of mayhem. Remember that friend I went to visit in Brittany? Well, he has an old gothic place about halfway between Mont St. Michel and the Loire Valley. You can't help but be afraid. How does the game work? Do you stay in character? Is it dramatic and morbid or more like slapstick?

I only have a couple of minutes before a co-worker arrives to pick me up. Sorry you didn't get the job. I hope we can remain pen pals, though. Lately our conversations have moved on to more inspiring topics than apartment-hunting in Paris.

As to your question about history, not only do I think it repeats itself, but I believe that it reaffirms & reinforces itself. I do think that these tides of history can be reversed by great humans, Jesus Christ or Gandhi, for example.

I was thinking that it would be great if we could exchange photos. As a show of trust and proof that you no longer believe me to be an axe murderer, you could send yours first. I know you said you didn't have a scanner, but I thought I might include a mailing address in Paris should you decided to mail me one. It's a neighbour's address (just in case your Evenings of Murder involve real corpses). I should mention that I barely know them, and I intend to rifle through their mailbox each morning until your photographs arrive. To spare my needless embarrassment, send them soon, will you :)

As for you, stop beating yourself up about your mother. It's one of those things that's unavoidable, leaving your parents. It would be worse if you stayed in Chéticamp and were miserable. Sometimes our parents can be pretty cagey about the whole thing, but I'm rather convinced that their primary concern is our happiness.

Oh, there's the doorbell, gotta go …

Terry

# Chapter 4
## City Girls

Tom's Little Havana was a nearby bar that doubled as a restaurant. After receiving Francesca's message I decided to go meet with her to hear so we could swap coffee shop stories. She was there meeting with the staff of the French school where she taught part-time and was also Vice-Principal.

Braced for the rain and wind, I wore my electric blue raincoat over my usual all-black attire. To my satisfaction, in the two and a half blocks that led to the bar, I managed to solicit half a dozen admiring glances from men. As I said, we all have our tragic flaws.

My family would have put it more succinctly, *T'es trop faraude. Crache en l'air, tombe sur le nez.* If it was indeed vanity I was spitting in the air, it was coming back down at me in buckets. All the same, Erotica (Neurotica's alter ego) pasted on a flirtatious smile and sauntered in.

Francesca was conducting the meeting as if she were waving her hands in front of a choir (or rather an orchestra). I chided myself for thinking of a choir. After all, I was done with all aspects even remotely related to religion.

This was one meeting Francesca was tired of. I could tell because she was saying things like, "I have the energy and the endurance to stay up all night," which she undoubtedly had.

Then, glancing at her watch and at the tired faces around the table, she added hastily, "But I realize that some of you have other commitments, so I think we should respect our proposed time limit and try to come to some consensus about how we are going to divide up this class."

A tall Nordic beauty, Francesca had long blond hair and piercing blue eyes. Even the sharpest observer would have difficulty in discerning her tendency to be overbearing. In this meeting, not only was her passion palpable to those interested in continuing the discussion but her remarks about respecting the group's needs touched those who were desperate to get home to their families. This latter group began gathering their papers.

"Before you leave, though, I want to remind everyone that we came here tonight with four possible options. I think we have eliminated at least two of them. Tomorrow, we will be meeting with both the parents and the students affected by these changes. We will present them with these two options, and in consultation with them we will finalize our plans." In other words, the option Francesca had decided on from the start would win the day.

She was almost at the crescendo; I could feel it coming in the same way I knew a *suête* was coming. She got up. "But wait, there is one last item before we adjourn …" she said, adding a wide smile, "Before you go, I want to thank you all, not just for tonight but for an amazing month of September. I couldn't have done it without each one of you. I have a little something for everyone, but you can't open it just yet. Go home and make yourselves a cup of herbal tea or some hot chocolate or pour a nice hot bath, and then open it."

Francesca, knowing full well that I had been watching her, turned at that opportune moment. "Isabelle. Hey, everyone, look who's here. You all remember Isabelle, don't you? Great timing, we were just wrapping up, right guys!" Who could ever say no to that?

After a few last quick hugs, Francesca ushered them all out except Sonya, the art teacher. Francesca always dropped her off after their meetings. Sonya was also in charge of the set design for the play my acting class was putting on.

Alone at last. There was a brief moment of silence as we watched the last ones climb the stairs and make their exit. "Well, thank God, that's over. I seriously need a glass of wine or something. You choose, Isabelle — it's my treat. Let's make it cognac. I know you like cognac. Sonya, do you like cognac?" But before Sonya could respond, Francesca turned to me, "Order us each a double. How are you, by the way. I'm so glad you could come. But wait, I have to run to the bathroom first."

As Francesca flew off in the direction of the washroom, I signalled the waiter, ordered three double Remys, and prepared to settle in by lighting one of my Indonesian cigarettes. I offered one to Sonya, who declined, adding that she was cutting back.

As usual, my choice of oral fixation elicited a few curious glances as soon as the distinct aroma of cloves began wafting through the room. Neither did I mind the attention. Besides, the smell always reminded me of Christmas and since that was a happy memory the scent quickly worked its charm. I sank with a slow smile into the leather chair. "So, Sonya, we never did get a chance to catch up during last night's rehearsal. How've you been?"

I thought of Gilles' earlier comment about passersby guessing that I was the artist and not he. No matter which stereotypical criteria were used, I was certain that Sonya would've been singled out as an artistic type in any crowd. Her red hair reminded me of a field of wild poppies and her casual gypsy-style clothing only added to the palette. Despite her flamboyant appearance, Sonya was always quietly personable, as if she had a secret unsung *joie-de-vivre*. She was in no way perky like Francesca. This was most evident in her long pauses when asked any question regardless of how simple it appeared on the surface. Then again, Sonya was one of the few people I knew who truly listened to questions and answers. Sonya was a poem. Her soft words were like cascading sonnets in an otherwise fast-paced world.

"How am I?" long silence, "Well, I guess I'm surviving, but the more I think about this business of teaching the more I wonder if I'm cut out for it," another longish pause, "Then again, I might be getting old and cynical."

I could certainly relate. I had a teaching interview in two days and was feeling much the same way. "That's right. Francesca mentioned something about you taking a masters class over the summer — art therapy, wasn't it?"

Before Sonya could come up with an answer, Francesca returned armed with a million questions about how my class at Dal was going and more importantly, how my first acting class had gone. If Sonya was a poem, Francesca was more of a dance, a step dance. Her liveliness infected me.

After four months in Chéticamp without my closest friends and the thrill of live theatre, I had been feeling *défilopée*, the stage when an item of clothing has threads hanging out from everywhere and is ready for mending. The acting classes and my friends were like expert seamstresses. I was like brand-new.

"We're putting on a play called *Smoke Damage.*"

"Uh hmm, so what's it about?"

"I'll be playing one of five women who take a vacation to Europe. The trip becomes some sort of quest." I was trying to sound *blasé* when, in fact, the way I began stressing almost every other word made it obvious how exhilarated I was by the whole thing.

"What kind of quest? What role will you be transforming into? Doesn't it sound fascinating, Sonya? You were saying earlier that you're doing the set, right? By the way, cheers, girls. Here's to phenomenal women!" We clinked glasses.

Sonya probably wouldn't have replied, so I forged ahead deliriously and forgot I was in the presence of poetry. "Yep, I think this will be one of the best plays I've been involved in yet, a quest about witches." Francesca overstated her curiosity then by lifting her eyebrows. She intended to show intense interest but I knew it meant she was struggling to keep her eyes open.

"Sounds good. When will you put it on? Sonya and I should bring the students ..." But she was cut off in mid-sentence.

"Well, well, well, what have we here ... I had a feeling we might track you down here."

My roommate Tony had obviously been out drinking. His brother, Calum, on the other hand, was always cool and charming regardless of alcohol consumption.

Immediately annoyed, I gave them an *oh, it's you* look. Since having reinstated the Red Table Society, Erotica, Neurotica and I had been practising my childhood looks. It was second nature. I knew they could be very enchanting, or as I hoped in this case, disparaging.

Tony was my toughest audience. Ignoring me, he plunged into the nearest chair. Wearing his favourite magician costume, Tony oozed with an *I don't give a shit* attitude. He didn't need a wardrobe to go along with it, since the scowl was self-explanatory. His brother, on the other hand, had quickly mastered a casually urbane look fit for the Maritimes. He was sporting a thickly knit pullover of tweedy natural colour, designer jeans, and a suede jacket. Definitely outdoorsy and not a look anyone would associate with a corporate accountant. He was the younger and more handsome of the brothers. At least, he was the most likely to end up on a magazine cover, not that this impressed me in the least.

Francesca saw their arrival as a cue for her to leave. She didn't like Tony and had hoped I would stay away from him after our four-month separation. She had been vocal in opposing my decision to let him stay in the apartment for a few more months. Tony and I were rather destructive together. Not that we were an actual couple or anything, but if truth be told we were more than friends.

"You three should stay and I should drive Sonya home so I can get some sleep tonight. I still have formula to make and Poppy will be awake at six or seven tomorrow." Poppy was Francesca's eight-month-old daughter.

I deliberately turned to include Sonya in the conversation. "Sonya, I've been meaning to ask you how your daughter Helen is doing?"

Tony interrupted Sonya's pause then. "Where the hell's the bar wench? I need a drink."

Taking my cue, Sonya ignored Tony as well. "Oh, you know Helen, she's taking Germany by storm."

*Bella and P'tit Pierre, who both enjoyed a drink in their day, were looking on.*

*— When are you going to start showing me what I supposedly don't know about, Mother?*

*— Patience, my son. We have all the time in the world, you and I. Isabelle must be able to live her own life, and besides, all of these characters will eventually lead her to my little secret.*

*— Speaking of characters, what do you make of that script she was talking about? You wouldn't have had a hand in that, now would you?*

*— Oh, a little nudge here, a little nudge there. Let us go on with the story, shall we?*

Francesca returned from having paid the bill. "Ready, Sonya?"

"Are you sure we can't persuade you to stay for one drink, ladies? I was hoping to get a chance to know you a little better ..." Calum flashed his perfect, white teeth in Francesca's direction and signalled the waiter to come over in that subtle upper class way he had.

Francesca ignored him with a smile. Turning to me with a hug, she whispered in my ear, "Have I told you in the last twenty-four hours how happy I am that you're back?"

"Fran before you whisk Sonya away I want to ask her a quick question." Turning to Sonya, "I know Fran mentioned my hooked rug and that paintings are more your field, but have you had a chance to think of anyone that might help me date it?"

"You're right. I don't know much about hooked rugs but you should go talk to the woman at the Farmer's Market who restores old rugs and tapestries. If she can't help you, I'll bet she might be able to tell you who can."

Calum wasn't ready to throw in the towel just yet. "Hey, is anyone psyched to go check out the autumn leaves around the Cabot Trail this weekend? Francesca, you could bring Poppy along too ..."

"We'll see. Right now I really have to go."

"Hey, wait a sec." I gave Francesca another hug. "We didn't get a chance to swap coffee shop stories. When you called you said something happened at a coffee shop today?"

"Oh, yeah, the coffee shop, I can't wait to tell you about this mystery man. He came into the café all decked out in an Armani suit and he ..."

"An Armani suit! Did you say an Armani suit? Are you positive it was Armani?"

"Yeah, I'm pretty sure, but what's so important about the suit? I was just going to say that ..."

"No, don't speak, don't speak." This had become one of my favourite affectations since I'd watched a Woody Allen movie with that line in it. "Wait and tell me tomorrow." As much as I was dying to hear about it I felt sure that Francesca would leave before I could get the whole story.

"Isabelle, you're acting even weirder than usual. Did some guy in an Armani suit attack you today or what?"

"No, no. It's nothing like that. Let's just get together tomorrow. Bring Poppy. I haven't seen her since Saturday."

Around this time, Tony's impatience peaked. He was *bouqué* like spoiled children get when they don't get any attention.

"Isabelle, why the hell do you drink here? It's too fucking pretentious. Look at all these goddamn suits. Can't we dump this place and go home to play a round of strip poker or something? We could pick up a pizza on the way?"

When this was met with an uncomfortable silence, Calum intervened on behalf of his older brother. "Oh, don't mind Tony, he's behaving terribly Orwellian tonight."

This time, I flashed Calum my chilly *yeah, whatever* look, then threw Tony a sharper and positively *Arctic ice chips from an igloo* look. Turning back to Francesca, "So, my day's wide open. When's good for you?"

"Well, I have that parent-teacher meeting tomorrow, but I should be done by lunch, and I don't have classes in the afternoon. How does a late lunch sound?"

"Fabulous, 1:30 good? How about Cheapside Café? You know, the place I love so much with the spectacular pumpkin walls in the art gallery?"

"Sounds good."

We hugged again. Francesca, shaking her head, said, "You really are acting strange tonight." But I knew that she enjoyed my penchant for melodrama and intrigue every bit as much as Erotica did.

"It was really nice seeing you again, Sonya. Sorry we didn't get a chance to talk more about that art therapy class. We should do that coffee soon, or maybe grab a quick supper together before the acting class next week?"

I was feeling a little bit guilty until a little voice inside my head reminded me that guilt was only one of a number of useless remnants from my Catholic upbringing. Kind of like those fruit flies that appear every summer and must be annihilated before they multiply. Besides, less than two weeks ago I had spent a great evening with Sonya during the film festival. *Hotel Splendide* was a visual feast and I had felt as complacent as a cat on the sunniest windowsill.

Eventually Sonya replied, asking if I was free tomorrow night. I said I had to prepare for a teaching job interview and wanted to spare her from the inevitable manic mood.

"Yeah, she'll probably take it out on me instead." Tony may have been drunk, but he never missed a beat.

Sonya and I agreed. Next week sounded fine. After a last round of hugs, Francesca and Sonya left. I turned my attention to my male companions. Noticing that my cognac had been replenished, I raised my glass, "Here's to Pierre Trudeau."

"Did you know that Denys Arcand's film *Stardom* was partly filmed in Trudeau's Montreal law office?" Along with being a successful accountant Calum took pride in his cultural savvy. Instead of leaving immediately, as Tony wanted, we spent the next half-hour debating Arcand's latest film. As far as I was concerned, the film itself was less of a topic for discussion than what I considered Arcand's arrogant and offensive address to the audience following the film's debut.

It was Tony and Calum's turn to shut me out of the conversation. My thoughts turned to arrogance. Even Francesca had a weakness for arrogance. Was it just a coincidence that I seemed drawn to vanity? It wasn't as if I was one to overlook people's tragic flaws. Reminded that assumptions of superiority were most often the flip side of low self-esteem, I knew this was more about my own struggle. Could I possibly find a solution by fighting the battle vicariously? Probably not.

Besides, there was a magical element to my friendship with Francesca, almost as if alchemy had had a hand in it. We met shortly after my devastating breakup with John, on the eve of Francesca's own marriage breakdown. One thing for sure, we both loved with a passionate, if not always compassionate, zeal.

A smile was slowly creeping its way back on my face as I conjured up an image of John and imagined his voice describing our failed relationship. "Going out with you was like going around the Cabot Trail at ninty miles an hour with no brakes."

Well, at least it hadn't been boring.

"Hey, what's that smile for? You look like you're having a sexual fantasy. Not that there's anything wrong with that ..." Tony liked Erotica.

"You mean as long as it's you she's fantasizing about, don't you?" Finally, a crack in Calum's polished veneer.

As we made our way back to the apartment, we passed Joe, the homeless man from the coffee shop. I couldn't resist going up to him and offering him a cigarette. It struck me as odd that he never asked me for money even when I could hear him asking those in front of me and behind me for change.

"Hey, miss, do you mind if I call you Venice? You look like a Venice."

I was taken aback momentarily but recovered quickly, "Sure, Joe. Have a nice night."

If Joe was surprised that I knew his first name, he hid it well.

As I hurried to catch up with the boys, I made a mental note to come back and talk to Joe someday soon. This reminded me of the man in the Armani suit — I was sure I recognized him from somewhere, but where was it? For the life of me, I couldn't remember.

Paris — October 1, 2000

Isabelle?

Where are you? Have you been swallowed up by weeds that overtook your garden while you were away?

I just stepped out on my terrace. The clouds are wild tonight, low and moving very quickly across the sky. Not fog or even smog but clouds with shape and texture. Haven't seen anything like it before in Paris. Mesmerizing …

Please write soon so I don't have to fly over to Canada to find you!!!

Worried, Terry

Halifax, 2000 — October 2nd

*Chère* Terry

I can't defend my tardiness, but I will say, in my defence, that I've been busy working and socializing since my return. I'd planned on taking two weeks off but, alas, my life never quite works out that way.

On the Monday following my arrival, I got a call from an old professor at Dalhousie University asking if I was interested in filling in for a last minute no-show. So, silly me, I agreed. Now, I am immersed in historical research again and brushing up on topics I had put on a back shelf. I won't bore you with the details.

I'm so thrilled to be back, Terry. My friends are the best(!!!) *AND* I've resumed my acting classes!!! We're putting on a play called *Smoke Damage*. My character's name Is Tart, a rebellious punk rocker who goes on a European bus tour. Anyway, we go to visit landmarks where millions of women were tortured and killed as witches between the 15th and 17th centuries, at least I think those are the right centuries. Whatever, the action sort of slips back and forth, connecting the parallel lives of modern women and women of the Middle Ages and the Renaissance.

Just imagine, if my hooked rug turns out to be really old, I might even connect with some Acadian women from the past. I was so excited about it, I wrote my first poem since high school:

Walked home from the Middle Ages
With a feeling of peace and calm
Under the steel-harsh lines
Of a dark impenetrable night.

In my bag is a dancing skirt of wildflowers.
I almost feel in step with myself again,
I want to throw my shoes and feel
the earth beneath my feet.
I reach out to the gypsy woman
wading in the ocean of my dreams.

But, I reach that same corner
to a flashing red hand
So I pick up the pace
Of the city girl again.

*Je t'embrasse*,
Isabelle

PS    Thought about your questions. Will answer them later. By the way, can I invite dead people to the dinner party? Who would be on your guest list? Gotta run, I'm meeting my best friend, Francesca. Hoping to run into the art teacher on her staff so I can get some answers about the hooked rug. It's still a mystery to this city girl.

# Chapter 5
## Sibling Rivalry

Agreeing to play Trivial Pursuit with Calum and Tony doesn't stand out as one of my wisest decisions. Those two had a long history of one-upping each other, and, that night, I was the prize apparently. It was degrading, and it marked the unofficial end of my unofficial relationship with Tony.

Tony had convinced Calum that we were platonic roommates, though. For his part, Calum was new to Halifax and candid about his desire to meet women. I just happened to be one of them. He saw no moral reason to conceal his interest and I had the sudden urge to spray the window sills with holy water. This was a ritual my mother would perform when she was waiting for a *suète*.

"So, Isabelle, what's the story behind all these faceless women?" Calum had been looking around and seemed to approve of the colourful bohemia. The apartment was undoubtedly mine and this was obvious by the lack of Tony's things, except his piano.

"What on earth are you talking about?" Tony demanded.

"The paintings, they're all women with no faces."

"That's such a crock of shit. I'm the fucking magician in our family. That makes me the expert at noticing obvious stuff which morons like you miss. Besides, look at that one. I painted it for her and it has a woman's face in it."

"Okay, I grant you she has a face. But it's a moot point. I challenge you to make out any of her features." Calum winked at me. He knew this was a low blow.

"Moot, moot, what's this fucking moot crap? What are you all of a sudden, a fucking lawyer? I'll tell you what you are …"

"Tony, please stop screaming. We do have neighbours, you know." My brain screamed *tu marches sur la corde raide* by intervening in a family dispute, but I went ahead and tiptoed along the tightrope.

"Like I give a shit about the neighbours ..."

"Hey, Tony, chill out, will ya, there's no excuse for talking to Isabelle like that ..."

But I was taking over by this point. "I know what you need, you need to sleep off ..."

I was hissing the words at Tony and commanding him to march. I crunched down the hallway behind him. The hallway led to his bedroom. He offered no resistance. Was Tony secretly grateful that I had given him a way out of a debate he might lose? After all, Tony knew that his brother could talk himself out of a hat, even a magician's hat.

As soon as I detected heavy breathing, I headed back into the living room. Calum looked like he was waiting to be besieged by a second charge of the light brigade. Maybe he didn't know Tony as well as I did.

"You actually managed to put him out of his misery. Hell, you're a woman of many talents." Calum seemed genuinely bewildered.

"You two are way too competitive," I whispered as I sat down at the other end of the sofa.

"Really now, and what do you think we were competing for tonight?"

I was trying to decide whether or not to ignore that last question when Tony stormed into the room, "I just want to tell you, Isabelle, that I'm sorry I yelled at you and that I love you." Before I could respond, he bent over and kissed me. The kiss was void of any real tenderness. Tony was marking his territory and nothing more.

"Tony, if you ever want me to speak to you again, you'd better get your goddamn ass to bed and stay there." But he was already gone and the next sound was the slam of the bedroom door.

*"J'en ai eu assez."* This confession forced my head to bow on the backrest with a sigh. Calum moved next to me. I didn't even stop him when he started stroking my hair. I felt depleted. In some

inexplicable surge of humanity, Calum chose not to take advantage of my vulnerability at that moment.

For a long time, we sat in silence. I didn't even try to stop the tears as they leaked out. It wasn't like me to allow someone to witness the volcano I'd kept a lid on for so many years as it began to rumble. But ever since returning to Chéticamp, I seemed to have lost the fortitude for containing any emotional pain.

• • •

Paris — October 2ᵗʰ, 2000

*Chère* Isabelle,

So glad to hear you're alive and well! Yes, feel free to invite dead people to your dinner party. I can already tell by your gracious nature that you would want to invite me as one of the six, but I insist you choose another. Though it would sound inviting, I'm sure to argue with the guests on some existentialist question.

As for me — must have a member from the Algonquin Round Table. How about the acerbic Dorothy Parker? And since I enjoyed *Le Petit Prince* so much, Antoine de St. Exupéry would definitely have to come. So two from the literary field already. I should try to create some variety ...

Since feminist philosophy is a passion, Simone de Beauvoir is a must ... brilliant, articulate and quite underrated, from what I understand. That's three. Oops, I guess I just inadvertently included another writer. How about a politician? Nixon should come: contemporary, notorious, with a vault full of secrets. Two more. An entertainer. Chaplin ... rags to riches, an innovator, physically comedic and cerebral all in the same package.

One more. A traveller. Someone to represent many cultures — multilingual. Someone who appreciates the arts. Someone who enjoys my humour. Someone with wild dreams. Someone to help clean up. I was originally going to invite George Sand, but she's also a writer. Besides, I've heard that she and Dorothy have issues.

Hmm … I wonder if they might spice up the dinner party with some fiery exchanges, possibly even a murder?

That's it … I have decided. No George Sand. Will you come to my dinner instead, Isabelle?

me


2000 — October 3rd: watching the sunrise …

*Chère* hostess,

Would love to attend your dinner party, just tell me where and when! Is there a dress code? I think you have drawn up a superb guest list. Can you make sure I am seated next to Chaplin? I'd like to get his reaction to a dream I just had!!

Calum, Tony's brother, is asleep on the couch across from me. Since you asked, my favourite animals are dogs. In fact, I've always wanted a chocolate lab and had planned on calling him Chocolate until you beat me to it. Now I might have to go back to my morbid teenage caprice of having two dogs and naming them Rigor and Mortis! About my wildest dreams … Hmmm … Not on your life, though I will say that I think ultimate reality may be involved …

Earlier today, I ran into an old neighbour (Gilles) from Chéticamp that got me thinking about my hooked rug again. When I came home tonight, I tried calling my sister because of a possible lead Gilles gave me — turns out I got her damn answering machine. Next, I tried Mam, who decided that Natalie, an artist who used to rent our upstairs flat must have hooked it. My gut feeling says she didn't.

Later on, I showed the rug to Calum and discovered an inscription on the back. It was so faded, we couldn't quite make it out. It looks like one word, but I can't say for sure. Calum also made an unsettling remark about my paintings and my hooked rug. I'll fill you in later when I've figured it all out.

I have a romantic notion that the hooked rug has a history I have been chosen to uncover. Only, I have a tiny fear inside me that attracts me and repels me all at once. I told John once (he's the ex I told you about) that fear was like life because it was real. I recall his laughing lovingly and telling me I was probably better off drinking at the bar.

Second, my six dinner companions at An Evening of Murder: I would invite you (of course), George Sand (surprise), Anaïs Nin, Gandhi, John Lennon and Jonathan Larson. The last person, in case you haven't heard yet in Paris, is the writer/producer of a New York Broadway Show called *Rent*, which is my current favourite. Don't you think it would be ironic if Gandhi ended up being the murderer? Check out the attachment from my journal re: Chaplin dream.

Here's a Jonathan Larson quote for you to ponder:

> "The opposite of war
> isn't peace.
> It's creation.
>
> *Viva la vie bohème!*"

— Isabelle

PS    See the my attached journal entry about the Chaplin dream.


It was around five in the morning, as the sun was about to say *bonjour* that I startled Calum awake with my laughter.

"It's good to see someone's in a better mood." Calum was quick to respond in a sleepy voice.

"Oh, Cal, I'm sorry, go back to sleep. I was just writing down a dream in my journal." We were on opposite couches now.

"I'm awake now. May as well come over here and tell me what you were dreaming about that was so funny."

I hesitated, but remembering how kind Calum had been the night before, I got up and padded over to his side of the living room.

Stretching out next to him, I began:

I was floating past the dining room on my way to take a bath when I noticed a dozen red roses on the table. Instinctively I knew they had been sent by my fans, so I paused to speak with them ... this is embarrassing.

"Go on, you've got me curious now." His look urged me to continue.

"All right," Avoiding his gaze, I continued straight from my journal:

I chatted gaily with the roses about who I would most like to share a bath with, and, in the end, I decided to bathe with the roses instead. They floated in the water with me, all one dozen of them, rubbing their velvet faces against my skin, sometimes prickling me with their tiny thorns. Acupuncture, I thought. Petals came loose only to be trapped in webs spun by spiders of soap. I pasted some of the wet rose petals on my nipples and then, as an afterthought, plastered one under my nose, like a comedian's moustache. *Springtime for Hitler*, I thought. I wondered about the fact that both Hitler and Chaplin had similar moustaches. I began to drift away from my entrancement as I shivered in the bath water, now turning cold. I stood up and, in the mirror saw my reflection. A parody of Charlie Chaplin with rose petals on his nipples. That's when I laughed myself awake ...

For a long moment Calum was silent and I began to wonder whether he'd fallen back asleep. A sideways glance assured me he was awake. He was looking at me with a smile that kept growing until his dimples stretched and eventually the smile reached his eyes. He was dangerously handsome.

"You are a very fascinating woman, Isabelle Desveaux. Will you marry me?"

"Very funny, Cal. You're not exactly the marrying type."

"Perhaps you're right, but if I were the marrying type, I think I'd want to marry a woman like you." Another long silence. "If I were the marrying type, would you marry me?"

"I think that is what you referred to last night as a moot point, was it not?"

"*Touché.*"

I sat up sensing that Calum was getting too cozy.

"Do you have any idea how much I want you right now?" He sat up too, reached over and gently kissed my eyelids.

"It would be wrong. I just can't hurt Tony like that." I had surprised myself. Saying the words out loud made my hidden feelings leap into the room. Neurotica was close behind.

"Tony doesn't have to know, does he?" This time Calum was testing me. He now knew that I was in love with his brother. Why hadn't he seen it before? Or worse, had he seen and ignored it?

"He'd know, believe me. And, even if he was a complete asshole last night, I can't just write him off." I arched my back and got up, casting aside any doubt about my decision. "I should go take a shower."

"Isabelle?"

"Yeah?"

"Save some cold water, will ya?" I couldn't detect any profound disappointment in his voice, just resignation.

*Bella and her son were watching the mailman, who made his route by starting on Isabelle's street, drop off a small package in her mailbox.*

*— What's in that package, Mother?*

*— How should I know?*

*Moments later, a second man shuffled over to the same mailbox and carefully tried fitting a larger parcel inside. He was about to give up, when Cliff showed up and offered to deliver it to Isabelle in person. Although there was no return address on either package, there was a name written on the larger one:* Gilles.

# Chapter 6
## The Two Packages

In my rush to meet Francesca for lunch that day, I forgot to check my mailbox. Tony woke up that morning looking like he'd spent the night on *la corde à linge* or *la ligne à butin* as we call a clothesline in Chéticamp. He and Calum appeared to have temporarily called a truce and left together in order to go for breakfast and then go shopping, or as heterosexual males were inclined to call it, 'pick up stuff'.

Tony would be leaving on Monday. He worked as a refitter on the offshore pipeline although his unrequited dream was to earn his living as a concert pianist. Most people couldn't imagine the virtuoso talent at Tony's fingertips when they saw him parading in his magician costume. But I had never heard anyone come near his passionate rendering of Beethoven's "Appassionata". It was one of his favourites. Hard to believe that someone who took such pride in his ability to belch and fart at will could make such sweet love to piano keys.

No matter what Francesca thought of him, I couldn't help wondering whether Tony was as much a virtuoso in bed. And Tony's radar had undoubtedly picked up on my curiosity, which was probably why he seemed so damned smug all the time.

Anyway, Tony always stocked up on books, CDs and the like before he went. He had left without one word of apology for the night before, which shouldn't have surprised me, but nonetheless, left me more annoyed with him than ever. At least I could comfort myself with the prospect that I would have the apartment to myself again.

For his part, Calum acted as though nothing had happened between us and only tried to pin me down on a promise that I would go to Cape Breton with them on the weekend. I ended up agreeing that if the weather cooperated, I might go.

As I stood by the window watching the brothers disappear down Spring Garden Road, I smiled when I noticed that even from above I could distinguish their personalities. Tony's orange bedhead was a sharp contrast to Calum's perfectly parted black hair. Erotica had the urge to run her fingers through the mountains and valleys of Tony's hair.

I marvelled at their seemingly effortless reconciliation. Perhaps it was the absence of this ritual sibling catharsis that explained the rigor mortis in many of the Acadian families I knew, not least of which was my own. I knew far too many families that were plagued by the cancerous growth of silent resentment and unspoken grudges. Unfortunately, when they eventually surfaced, there was no radiation treatment that could eradicate the years of poisonous absorption in their bloodstream.

I considered, bitterly and half-seriously, that I could return to university and present a thesis proposing that the high rates of cancer in that sector of the population were due to the ever-present *rigor mortis* in the dead tissue of living beings! As I considered how mortified my mother would be by this idea, I lit a cigarette and turned on my laptop. I placed the cigarette gingerly in the sensual curve of the blue blown-glass ashtray on the coffee table. The ashtray had originally belonged to Pépére, then to my father, and now it was my only tangible souvenir of Pépére. On second thought, I would have to abandon my sinful habit in order to be taken seriously.

•   •   •

Paris — October 4th, 2000

*Chère* Isabelle,

I have a confession to make, but first. We must have been sending messages about the same time last night. I enjoyed your rose petalled nipple dream. I'm not so Freudian as to offer an interpretation, except that it's the product of a whimsical imagination. Have you ever walked in your sleep? I did as a child. Strange phenomenon. I doubt I do this any more, though its remnants still exist in rare waking dreams, where I catch myself briefly acting out the remainder of a dream.

It would have added an interesting component if your rose petal nipple dream had been in waking form. You notice where I'm placing my emphasis with reference to your dream, but I have already warned you of the lascivious nature of my mind.

I've been thinking about these murder nights you were telling me about.

When my siblings and I were young, our eccentric Uncle Fabien offered us $50 if one of us would spend the night in a haunted house in the woods of Les Laurentides. I was quite a skeptic, even then. After a few liquid spirits, Mon Oncle Fabien would always start with all the talk of fantômes and I was less than diplomatic in challenging his beliefs. Thus the offer was born. Unfortunately he revoked the offer at a more sober moment.

Anyway, there is a very ominous wine cellar at my friend's mansion. As a second option, we could murder people there. Do you believe in ghosts? It might explain the dreams you've been having. I wish I did. It would make life more interesting and scary. Scary can be a lot of fun.

Okay, I'm delaying. My confession: Isabelle, I really hope this won't make you want to end our friendship, but the thing is I am a GAY, which does not mean I have any expectations where you're concerned. I expect friendship, no more, no less. Please forgive my not telling you before, but of the responses I received on that pen pal web site, yours seemed like the most interesting. When I didn't tell you immediately, I started worrying how you might take it.

Please send a message soon to reassure me that all is not lost. Meanwhile, I'll take a look at your dinner guests again. I may have questions. I did notice I was invited, which I predicted in my earlier message. Not bad, huh. I am very, very sorry.

*Ton ami,*
Terry

PS     You've been holding out on our original pact: Nova Scotia, Acadians?

·      ·      ·

"Francesca, have you ever noticed that all the paintings on my walls have women with no faces in them?" Francesca and I were sitting outside in the courtyard. While his tempestuous relatives were amusing themselves elsewhere, the sun had decided to make a grand entrance.

"Not really. Why do you ask?"

"Cal made a remark about it last night and it's been bugging me ever since. It doesn't even make sense. I mean, if I had bought them all, you could say it was some weird fixation of mine, but many of the paintings were given to me. Like Tony's and that one you brought me back from your trip to Mexico. Then there's my most recent addition, though not a painting *per se*, also the image of a woman's back. Remember that hooked rug I found in the attic in Chéticamp?"

"Yeah, that is strange, unless the people giving you the paintings were cast under a spell … Didn't you say you were playing a witch in this play you're in?"

"No, I didn't. But since this is a class, we don't have real understudies. We do double up on roles in case somebody gets sick. My understudy role is Rebecca, the witch."

"Did you ever find out anything about that hooked rug?"

"Nada. I'm baffled."

"What did your mother say?"

"Mam thinks that an artist who rented the upstairs apartment hooked it, but I'm not convinced. It seems much older than some fifteen years."

"Is it possible that conditions like mould in the attic might have aged it faster?"

"Uhm, there's no mould in the attic, but it may be the heat, I don't know … Still that doesn't explain why it was in a tube with my name on it, or my grandmother's name."

"Coincidence?"

"That's my mother's take on it, but my gut is telling me it was meant for me. Period. Other than that, I have nothing to go on."

"You should bring it down to the market and show it to that woman Sonya mentioned the other night."

"That's exactly what I'm planning to do this weekend. In fact, it might be just the excuse I need to get out of Calum's Cape Breton excursion."

The waiter delivered our meals. Since I had decided to stay home to read my script rather than join Calum and Tony for breakfast, I had forgotten all about eating. The aroma of ginger rising from the plate immediately took my mind off faceless women.

"Speaking of fixations, what was all that about an Armani suit last night?"

"Oh, no, you don't, Fran, you go first. Remember, you're the one who called and dragged me out in the rain last night, so you could tell me about it and then abandoned me to the likes of Cal and Tony."

"Hey, you're the bozo who let him stay in your apartment. And judging by the way Cal was looking at you, I don't think he minded."

When I didn't reply in typical two second or less banter, Francesca continued, "Besides, you were acting so strange last night. I think my little episode with the police at the house …" I arched my eyebrow with concern. "Don't worry, nothing bad happened." Francesca took a bite of her salad.

"Police?"

"Yesterday morning I decided to correct some papers at Perks. You know how getting any correcting done at home with Poppy is next to impossible? I called Barb to come over and babysit for a few hours. I mean, you know how good I am? I always leave phone numbers and I even told Barb where I'd be in case she needed me."

"Uh hmm." I nodded assertively and repeatedly, giving Francesca the required look to affirm that she was a good mother. She had started using rising inflections at the end of her sentences and making questions out of statements. This quirk irritated me and I began drifting into an internal dialogue with Neurotica. *What were Calum and Tony talking about? Would Calum reveal my secret? And what about Terry being gay? Why was she telling me now?*

"I'd just started marking when this guy in an Armani suit came bursting in. He was apparently late meeting someone who was sitting at the table next to mine. He was ranting and raving about how someone had stolen his newspaper and how the world was going to shit when a man couldn't even get his own damn newspaper without being attacked. To make a long story short," Francesca paused to let me know she had noticed my inattention, "if I'd stayed there one minute longer I think I would have told the guy off."

It must have been the same guy! Where did I know him from? I was about to say something when she cut me off.

"Wait, there's more. It's a good thing I didn't lose it, since I hadn't seen the last of him yet. I just got up and went to Tim's down the street where it was quieter, and finished my correcting there."

"Are you dragging this out on purpose, or are you going to tell me when the police got involved?"

"How is everything, ladies?"

"Fine." My *look* was all the waiter needed for a reply.

"Isabelle, you didn't have to bite his head off."

"I didn't bite his head off."

"Isabelle, did you and Tony have a fight last night?"

"No. And, I don't want to talk about Tony. When did the police go to your house?"

"In other words, you did fight." Francesca noticed that the look hadn't left my face and was getting stormier. She switched gears. "Actually, the police didn't come to my house, they were at Craig's mother's house." This was getting more complicated by the minute.

"Gotcha. The police went to Craig's mother's house, and they were there because…?"

Over lunch, Francesca explained the whole sordid story. Because Craig's parents were out of town attending a family funeral, Francesca and Craig (and Poppy) were staying at their house to feed the dog and to field any urgent business calls. Meanwhile, Francesca's babysitter, who wasn't used to the place, had locked herself and the dog outside because of an automatic lock that she wasn't aware of.

With Poppy inside and no change to make a phone call, Barb, the babysitter, ran to the coffee shop where Francesca was supposed to be correcting papers. Since by this time Francesca had left (due to Armani man) and Barb had no idea where, the very thought that Poppy could be stranded (albeit, safe in her crib) for hours, sent Barb into a clear state of panic. Rather than ask anyone for help, she ran back to the house to check on Poppy (by peering through the window) and found her awake and looking like she was about to shriek. Barb then ordered the dog to guard the window and set off running yet again, this time to the school where Francesca taught, just in case she might find her there.

The secretary at the school, who was very calm and rational about such things, took control of the situation and proceeded in what she had considered the most appropriate fashion. She advised Barb to return to the house and stay there while the school telephoned Francesca's list of emergency contacts, who might know of Francesca's whereabouts or possibly even have spare keys to the house. The secretary had even reassured Barb that if for some reason no one was available, she would contact the police and send them to the house immediately.

Unfortunately, the secretary was unaware of one crucial detail: When all other avenues failed her, she sent the police to the wrong house.

"Which is how the police and this guy in the Armani suit ended up at Craig's parents', sitting at the table with Barb and me, drinking tea and writing a report about what happened."

"Holy shit." By this time the waiter had gotten up the nerve to make another appearance and the bill was sitting on the table ready to be paid. I reached for my purse. "I'm paying today, since it was my idea."

"No, you're not. You don't have a full-time job yet and besides, I didn't keep my end of the bargain and bring Poppy along. I figured she'd had enough excitement for one week. Craig's off work today, so he's with her."

"Francesca, come on …"

"Nope. Here's the deal. If you land that job tomorrow, you can pay for both Poppy and me next time."

"Speaking of tomorrow, I should really get my ass home soon and prepare for this interview."

As she was getting up to leave I gave her one of my looks.

"What?"

"What the hell was the guy with the Armani suit doing with the police!"

Francesca sat back down.

"See, that's what's so weird about the whole thing. I have no idea what he was doing there. And you know me, I usually ask a million questions. But yesterday I was so upset about what happened, I didn't find out a thing about him. Apparently I also have partial amnesia, 'cause if he introduced himself, I have no idea what he said. I didn't really give a shit until you started asking all those questions about him. So, what gives?"

"It's probably nothing. I think I saw the same guy getting his newspaper stolen. I recognized him from somewhere but I still can't place him. I wonder if he was reporting Joe when the police got the call to go to your house?"

"Joe? Who's Joe?" By this time we were walking out of the café, arm in arm.

"He's the guy who stole his paper."

"You know the guy who stole his paper?" We rounded the corner to where Francesca's car was parked.

"No, not exactly. I found out his name after it happened. It's not really all that important."

Before Francesca could ask more questions or revisit the situation with Tony, I blew her a kiss and darted down the street, calling over my shoulder, "Thanks for the lunch, Fran, and give a big sloppy kiss to Poppy for me."

"Hey, good luck on the interview. Call me the minute you're back."

On the way home I thought about how unlikely it was that a police officer would bring along a person reporting a crime to another crime scene. It didn't make sense. Then again, a lot of things weren't adding up these days.

But I didn't have time to think about it. I had an interview to angst about, not to mention a friendship that was beginning to drift apart and a secret that could change everything. I had promised myself a long time ago that I would only allow men in my life as long as I didn't care about their leaving. Tony's impending departure was threatening to ruin all that. Even worse was that Erotica and Neurotica's attempts at sabotage the night before had only managed to make it messier.

The minute I noticed a package in my mailbox, I ran over to investigate. In doing so, I almost collided into my neighbour Cliff who was coming around the corner. In defiance, Neurotica immediately appeared to remind me that I hadn't returned Cliff's last phone message. Turned out, he wanted only to deliver a second package that he claimed a friend had dropped off that morning.

He also took the opportunity to establish his ground rules. It appeared that having Gilles and Joe sit at his designated table had upset him greatly. I had to inform my friends that it was unacceptable for them to sit at *his* café table between 10 AM and noon. Secondly, that noncompliance to his first rule could bring them bad Karma and have a devastating impact on humanity since these were the exact hours that he recomposed the events of the last twenty-four hours into an epiphany for social revolution.

I thanked him for the package, agreed to pass on his advice, sent Neurotica packing and darted in my apartment to avoid any more of Cliff's *Bizarro World* counsel. Safe inside, I raced upstairs with my packages. I was surprised by both return addresses. One with no address at all, and the other simply read *Gilles*. I couldn't imagine what either box contained. "What the…?"

I was drawn to the larger one, which was marked *Fragile — do not bend*, so I tried to be as careful as possible. There was lots of wrapping and then a note. Normally, I would head straight for the prize, but, in case there were instructions of some sort, I decided to read the note first:

Dear Isabelle

    It was so nice to run into you again after all these years. I guess I should tell you straight away that my father passed away yesterday — he died peacefully in his sleep. Last night, I ended up in the attic looking for photographs for the memorial and I found this canvas. I thought about what you said. Since it was only gathering dust in a box in Adilia's attic, I thought you might get some enjoyment out of it. Hope you still like it.

    Just so you know, the memorial will be at 10 AM. Friday morning (at Snow's on Windsor Street — across from Sobeys). Of course, you're welcome to attend but please don't feel that you have to.

    I've been walking around all night thinking. I hope my note is coherent. I know you're busy and I don't want to bother you, but, on the off chance you have time, we could have that coffee. I would like to show you something my father left behind. I'm so tired that I will have to reread them but I think you might find a clue to your hooked rug in all this.

Take care,
Gilles

Inside the box was the painting of a sunflower, exactly how I remembered it. Finally I could hang up an image that wasn't the rendering of a woman, faceless or not. If there was anything sorcerous going on, this could be a sign that the spell was wearing off.

    As for the memorial, I couldn't decide what was the right thing to do. Memorials implied memories and I was still searching for mine. I knew they were *rapilotées* somewhere in my brain, but I had squashed them into such a tiny space that I couldn't locate them. What if all those terrible moments at my father and brother's funerals found their way out of the fog and came crashing into the present while I was at someone else's memorial? This fear had prevented me from stepping foot in a funeral home ever since. A decision for later.

I turned my attention to the second package. It was a very small box, about three inches wide, five inches long and no more than two inches thick. The moment after unwrapping the packaging and opening the lid, I shrieked in terror. There, nestled in a bed of mouldy moss, was a single, severed finger. Upon closer examination I realized that it was a plaster cast of a human finger. On the back of the lid, was written:

Don't forget — Halloween Dinner & Séance — Sonya's Haunted House — October 30, 8 PM — RSVP.

Halifax, 2000 — October 6th

*Chère* Terry,

Sunshine is pouring through my large living room windows in waves of intoxicating paradise. Today, I'm a hedonist whose sensuality has been ignited, unchaste and unrestrained, yet, all my pleasures are confined within the boundaries of my mind.

I awoke
to moonlight flooding through
my triptych of windows
shimmering trinity
casting dancing lovers,
across my floor,
reflecting an old love story
on the walls.

If I'd stayed awake much longer
I would have heard the crash
of the waves and the lift
of the wake
concussing with the beating pulse
of mad hearts in
the heat of possession.

I prayed to the angels,
who descended,
and, sprinkling my eyelids
with their miraculous dust,
released me and carried me
through the gates and
into my garden of dreams.
        — Isabelle

I haven't forgotten your question, "How do you feel about being Acadian?" I think I am avoiding that one for fear of what the answer might dredge up from the sewer in my brain. I can almost smell a stench in the air as I write to you now.

I don't know why, but ever since I began writing to you, all these memories from a past I considered over with are resurfacing. At first, they were mostly about John, but now there are others.

Mixed in with these memories are stranger and stranger dreams. Last night, instead of sleeping I felt as though I'd gone to the movies. I wasn't even part of my own dreams — I rather felt as if I was observing someone else's. They were rather drab movies too. In one of them a woman just sat at a frame, hooking a rug. I was so engrossed in trying to figure out who she was that I forgot to look at the actual rug she was working on. Could this possibly be the rug I found in the attic? Or am I simply losing my mind?

Here's the weird part. The woman never looked up at me but I felt like she was composing a message for me in her hooked rug. Then at certain moments in the dream, I felt like I was almost tumbling inside her brain but the images there were so scary that I would half shake myself awake and then start the voyage back towards her. I feel crazy saying this, but ever since I started this play, I feel like there's someone trying to pull me into another century. This woman may appear harmless sitting at her frame, but I think it's her, whoever she is …

About the whole omission thing, STOP WORRYING!! I want us to remain pen pals. Besides, even though I don't think I've outright lied, I may have exaggerated my scintillating personality in my intro, so if you can accept me as the regular Jane that I am, I would love for us to see where this strange friendship will take us. From now on, let's be honest, okay?

I'm on my way to a memorial service — I think I told you about running into an old neighbour (Gilles). It's his father's memorial today.

Still your friend,
Isabelle

Paris — October 8, 2000

*Chère* Isabelle,

I was so surprised to hear your voice on our answering machine. Too bad I missed your call. At least now I know what you sound like. I had an artist friend develop a composite based on previous emails and the voice recording. He's quite talented, but all his renderings tend to look like Juliette Binoche, so I can't put much faith in them.

By the way, I read every word in your last email in complete agony until I reached the part where you let me off the hook. I kept expecting the axe to fall, but I should have trusted my first instincts. I am really enjoying getting to know you, Isabelle — but your honest confession of being a plain-Jane is the most preposterous lie yet. I think that John was a very lucky man when he was with you but also the craziest man to have let you slip away.

About Acadian history, I've been doing some casual research of my own here at the Sorbonne library. If ever you feel inclined to talk about it, I will be all ears (or eyes), but in the meantime do you know anything about the area around the university where I will be teaching? In case you forgot, it's called Université Sainte-Anne.

Our chats are becoming like a chain letter. I'm figuring you'll be the first to break, even though your writing capabilities exceed mine.

One of my brothers and a cousin are arriving in Paris for a visit next week. I'll be in and out of town for awhile, but will try to get a current photograph while they're here and send it to you. Isabelle, if I haven't said anything about your memories and dreams it's only because I don't know what to say. Yet ...

Sweet dreams,
Terry

# Act Two: Erotica & Neurotica
*Stage a Coup de Théâtre*

*Props:* an enchanted mirror, a crystal ball and a ghost or two ...

# Chapter 7
## Through the Looking Glass

On October 29, I woke up and the sun was sparkling. I could hear a man shouting at someone on the street below. "You're a good-for-nothing piece of horse shit. Fuck you!"

The female voice that responded was *vite sur ses patins*, quick on her skates. "Oh, yeah. Well, you're nothin' but a bucket a piss, and, besides, yer mother hates ya."

The sun kept streaming in through my bedroom window like incandescent beams of club soda. Paradoxes. They're at the core of life, aren't they?

October 29 also marked the beginning of my seventh week of part-time work. I hadn't succeeded in bewitching the interviewers enough to hire me for a full-time teaching job. Even though the odds were stacked against me (another qualified candidate was already working in the school), I was crushed by this perceived failure. I couldn't decide what the situation was straining most, my pocketbook or my sanity.

Even the acting classes weren't enough stimulation to satisfy my constant need to be consumed. Some days, I couldn't stop the feelings of non-accomplishment swell over me, and in their wake, other more neurotic emotions would seep into my psyche. Yesterday I had gone so far as to convince myself that the whole world hated me. It was obvious that even my so-called friends were only putting up with my antics because they felt sorry for me.

Everyone except Calum. With Tony out of the picture, Calum was the one person vying for my provocative, if somewhat manic companionship. Calum knew I could never love him and like me, he was probably looking for someone he could leave without a clutter of emotions. But even Calum's persuasive charm was no match for my misplaced sense of loyalty. I would never betray Tony. That is to say, I never slept with his brother. Where was I in all this mess?

Due to my foul mood, I almost called Sonya to back out of my assigned role in the Halloween dinner party. But in the end I was able to gain enough perspective to recognize the familiar surroundings. I had described it once to a therapist (another short-lived affair) as entering the belly of Jonah, the neurotic whale. This was the place I had entered and remained, for a long time after my father and brother died. This time Jonah let me escape after only a couple of weeks of self-loathing. I swam out eagerly and immediately packed my bags.

Before leaving the apartment, I took one quick look in the hall mirror. Hand firmly planted on hip, I addressed the reflection sharply, "Now, Neurotica, you will be staying home this weekend. Got it?"

Calum was supposed to be picking me up as soon as he finished auditing one of the departments he was working on. This could be as early as after lunch or as late as six or seven. One thing I had to do before he picked me up was to figure out a costume, since the dinner party was based on the board game An Evening of Murder. For the first time in days, I was dressed and out the door by the time the shops had opened up on Spring Garden Road.

Since we would be staying at Sonya's house on the south shore for the weekend, I decided to start by looking for gourmet treats, preferably in ghoulish disguises. When most of the grocery shopping was out of the way, I headed to the second-hand shops to scour the racks for possible costumes.

With my improved mood I was also feeling creative and soon found myself spending much of the morning intent on developing my roles for *Smoke Damage*. The week before, what was supposed to have been my understudy role had become a second permanent role. The woman who was supposed to play the part of Rebecca, the witch, had dropped the class. And now, even though my two characters were worlds apart, I was finding it increasingly difficult to keep them separate in my mind.

I spotted a mauve dress that appealed to my romantic side, a persona that seldom made her appearance. The dress was flowing and satiny. The inside tag said it was made in France. Although it was completely inappropriate for the Evening of Murder, I felt compelled to try it on. As I walked towards the dressing room I glanced in a side mirror and noticed an odd twinkle in my eye. I kept walking, but with each step I took I began feeling as though I were spanning decades if not centuries. It was the strangest feeling ...

•    •    •

"You can imagine how shocked I was when I saw her reflection." I confided to my companions.

"All right, which is it, are you trying to fool us into forgetting about this damn fog or are you putting us in the mood for Halloween with this tale of yours?" Calum stared straight ahead as he tried to follow what little of the road remained visible.

"Neither. I swear, when I looked into that mirror, another woman was there. I couldn't really make out her face, but she had darker hair than mine."

"Was her body different than yours?" Calum was probably on another one of his fishing expeditions, but I wasn't about to be derailed.

"Well, for one, her body looked like she had given birth to many children. She wasn't fat, but her skin was looser and had stretch marks."

"What about her breasts?" This time Calum made no effort to conceal his intentions and offered a suggestive glance in my direction. By this time, I had decided that since I had sent Neurotica back to the apartment, it was Erotica's turn to come out and play a little.

"They were rounder and fuller than mine, but they also went separate ways like a swimmer's breasts, kind of like they had a mind of their own. Am I painting a clear enough picture for you, Calum?"

"Uh hmm, so what do you make of this outrageous story, back there, Gilles?"

"Sounds to me like Isabelle had a vision. It's probably not as uncommon as people would like to think it is." At least someone believed me.

I began to worry again about how Gilles would get along with my friends. When Sonya had called in a panic because one of the guests couldn't come, I suggested on impulse that Gilles might like to come along. Since he was new in Halifax, it seemed like the perfect way to thank him for the painting and to get his mind off his father's death. Now I wasn't so sure how brilliant my idea had been.

"Gilles, I hope you'll like my friends. Sonya is the art teacher you met the other day at Timothy's and she's the host. Did she call you by the way? She was supposed to get a hold of you to explain the game and your role."

"Yeah, she called me."

"And, Francesca, who teaches at the same school as Sonya, is my best friend. She's from Sweden and her partner Craig is British, though you would never guess by his accent. He worked in the Marines for years before coming to Canada. He was stationed in Ireland during most of his time and left because the tension was too high. Now he sounds more like a Cape Bretoner than anything. I think he's rebelling against his formal upbringing. Doesn't mince his words. But he and Francesca really are a great couple. They have a nine-month old baby, Poppy. She's adorable."

"Doesn't sound like the kind of guy Francesca would go for. She seems kinda conservative under that bubbly exterior." This was a perceptive observation coming from Calum. Sometimes he surprised me.

"As a matter of fact, they have a romantic history. They first met years ago when Francesca was studying French in Paris. They were pen pals for a long time, but after Francesca got married to a Canadian and moved here, they lost touch. I like to think it was fate that brought them back together not long after she divorced her first husband."

"Isabelle, who would of thought when you were terrorising the neighbours in Chéticamp that underneath all that was a hopeless romantic."

"I'm not romantic at all, Gilles, I just want my friends to be happy."

"Terrorising the neighbourhood?"

"Oh, it's nothing, just a little temper tantrum I had once involving Gilles."

"Isabelle, did you find out anything about that hooked rug you mentioned the last time I saw you?" Gilles asked.

"No. I tried to call my sister, but no luck 'cause she's away on a course. Remember that woman you mentioned? Yvette? You wouldn't know if she's by any chance related to Etienne Leblanc? I went home last week for Mom's birthday and she told me that he's the man Pépére bought the house from."

"I'll say they're related, that's her grandfather. Now that I think of it, I think that's how she and your sister started hanging out. Yvette was used to visiting her grandparents at the house and she kept hanging around even after your grandparents bought it."

"Do you know if her parents or grandparents used to hook rugs as well?"

"Yeah, but only the women. Her grandmother and mother were some of the best known rug-hookers in Chéticamp. But I can tell you one thing for sure. Neither of those two were hooking naked women. They were both as chaste as the Virgin Mary herself."

"You know what they say about appearances being deceiving ..." Calum reverted to his usual persona of clichés and chauvinism.

"Uh, not in this case. So, how old is your mother now, Isabelle?"

"She just turned seventy. I surprised her on the morning of her birthday by showing up for breakfast with seven long-stem roses. I told her she'd get the full dozen when she turned a hundred and twenty."

"You must have left in the middle of the night to make it there for breakfast?"

"Yep. We left Halifax around four in the morning, Calum, me and Tony, Calum's brother. Tony's also my roommate. It was one of my crazy impulses, but Mam was giddy with delight when we arrived."

My mother had also made no effort to conceal that Tony was her favourite of the brothers. The fact that he tuned her old piano and could play anything she requested made him a star in her eyes. For a loner, Tony managed to become quite charming with older women. He and my mother flirted outrageously all that weekend. I wasn't jealous, though. I hadn't seen her seem so alive since Dad passed away.

"Speaking of roses, Calum, I never did get the chance to thank you for those roses you left on my dining room table."

"What roses?"

"The ones with the note that said they wanted to take a bath with me. You are the only person who knew about the dream."

"I didn't leave those. Tony did. I guess I told him about your dream. I hope it wasn't supposed to be a secret."

Although I liked to think I was a duplicate of my father, my gift for worrying was most definitely a trait inherited from my mother. As we drove on through thicker and thicker fog, I gave full vent to that gift.

It was close to midnight when we pulled in the driveway. I yawned and glanced apologetically at Calum as the light in the car came on.

"I'm sorry, I must've dozed off. How did you find the house without my directions?"

"A: I'm a fairly self-sufficient kinda guy, and B: Gilles is a talented instruction-reader." We were unloading the trunk when Francesca appeared in the doorway.

"Hey, you guys, thanks to God you're here. I was about to call the police to send out a search party." Francesca was also a gifted worrier.

"Do you guys need help bringing stuff in? Actually," Francesca directed her next words over her shoulder, "Craig, get your shoes on and go help them."

Once Calum had given Gilles and Craig some stuff to bring inside, he profited from the few moments we had alone before heading in. He reached for my arm and drew me close to him.

"Just don't forget how self-indulgent I become when I see you waking up with those bedroom eyes of yours." He slowly began to tease my lips with his own until he noticed that I wasn't resisting. I was determined to erase those damn roses from my head.

"Isabelle, do you guys need any more help out there?" Some days Francesca was just so damn helpful it was maddening.

"No, we're good. I was just looking for the bag with the cognac in it, in case we want a nightcap." Francesca wasn't going anywhere, so we headed inside. I could've sworn I heard a distinct growl coming from Calum.

"Hey, Isabelle, did you notice the clothesline?" I turned and, squinting through the fog, discerned a row of ghostly figures floating eerily above Sonya's rose bushes.

"What on … well, if that doesn't beat the cake! They're awesome. They look so real in this fog, like ghosts. Who put those up?"

"Sonya, of course." With a shiver, I ran up to the house to congratulate Sonya on the phenomenal display. Francesca caught up to me at the doorstep and gave me a hug.

"Cognac, my ass. Don't think for a minute I didn't see that kiss out there. What gives?"

"Not now, maybe later … Hey, has everyone met Gilles? Remember, Francesca, how I told you about this neighbour I ran into at the coffee shop last month."

I was about to walk into the house when a familiar scent in the air made me turn to look at the clothesline again. There she was. It was the woman from the dressing room. She waved and disappeared into the sheets before I could tell anyone to look.

"Isabelle hurry up or you'll catch your death. You should be wearing a coat."

"Francesca, can you smell hyacinths?"

"Isabelle, it's October. Hyacinths bloom in the spring silly. Now get in." But I was positive the sweet smell in the air was that of hyacinths.

— *Mother, you're going to make Isabelle think she's losing her mind. First Patronille, now the hyacinths.*

— *My son, Bella began, but was interrupted by an unexpected voice.*

— *Did I hear my name, Patronille asked.*

— *Yes my dear, said Bella, my son here is upset that I have sent you to greet my granddaughter.*

— *Well, that's easy for him to say, said Patronille, he hasn't been forgotten yet.*

— *Exactly what I was thinking, Bella agreed. Besides, my son, Patronille had to appear at some point. I thought adding her signature scent was divine inspiration. Now do you want to know the whole story, or not?*

— *You know I do, but I don't understand what Patronille has to do with it.*

— *And this is why, my son, I am telling the story and not you. Shall I continue?*

# Chapter 8
## A Clue from the Past

"Hi, Gilles. Name's Craig — I'm Francesca's better half. So sorry to hear you had to grow up with that demon next-door."

Gilles said hello and asked to be directed to the washroom. Sonya led him away.

"What's this I hear again about you being a demon?" It didn't take Calum long. He was already taking over the kitchen, bringing out glasses and opening bottles.

"C'mon you guys, let's move into the living room, so you can warm up by the fire, and so we can talk." Francesca clearly enunciated her last word in my direction. I pretended to notice the house and not Francesca.

"Holy shit, Sonya has done amazing work on the house since I was last here."

"Thanks for noticing." Sonya walked back in. She asked if we were hungry and we told her about our little detour to pick up scallops and chips in Hubbards.

"Aren't scallops supposed to be aphrodisiacs, or is it shrimp?" This time, Calum picked up on Francesca's meaning. I flashed her a look, but Francesca remained wide-eyed, smiling beguilingly. Gilles walked back in, looking relieved.

"Gilles, tell us why Isabelle broke your windshield." Francesca must have told Craig about that little episode.

"She came racing over the moment I drove up with my first brand-new car and demanded that I take her for a test drive. That's what she called it, a test drive. She used to come up with these expressions that she heard adults use and she wanted to try them out.

Anyway when I said no, she said she'd throw the biggest rock at the car unless I took her on a test drive immediately. I don't think she even gave me the opportunity to answer. I must have paused, which she took for a no, and so she did exactly as she'd promised: picked up the biggest rock on the ground and threw it straight through the windshield before anyone could stop her."

Gilles had started talking at his usual frantic pace, but when he noticed that everyone was listening attentively to his story, he began to slow down. Even his thick accent seemed to recede.

"I think that was around the same time you stole the two rabbits from preschool. You were really on a roll that year."

"See, I told you she was evil. Gilles you're probably from a good Acadian Catholic family. Were they going nuts with the holy water when they'd see Isabelle heading over from next door?" I knew Craig was taunting me, but, by then, I was already wrangling with Neurotica who had materialized out of nowhere.

"To be honest, she wasn't all bad. Even I'll admit that. We all had our stories about Isabelle. One of the cutest things she ever did was when our little brother, Pierre, died in a car accident. She rushed over to help before anyone could stop her and, assessing the situation, ran straight to my sister Adilia, who was beyond herself with grief. Without batting an eyelash, she told Adilia very sincerely, "Don't cry Adilia, Pierre isn't all dead, he's only dead a little bit." You can imagine how that one made us shake our heads at little Bella in later years after the horror of the situation had passed. But you know, to be fair, after she said it, she just sat and hugged Adilia until her father showed up and carried her home."

"He's only dead a little bit?" Calum laughed, but got up and casually walked over to the couch. "Move over you two, make some room for a tired chauffeur. What was that name again, Little Bella?"

I saw Francesca register the look in his eyes as Calum teased me. I suddenly felt like I was being tested and didn't like it one bit.

"Yeah, we called Isabelle 'Little Bella' to distinguish her from her grandmother who was also named Bella. Now there was a strange bird, that one. A true *Piquin*, if ever there was one."

I told them about Mémére Bella and how she used to swear that eccentricity was just another word for being aware of life's ineffable secrets.

"Well, that might explain — what shall we call it — your individuality?" Craig was relentless. "Calum did you know that Isabelle believes in ghosts and in reincarnation?"

"Yeah," I said, "which is why I'm leaving all my money to myself in my will. It's so you won't get any. Besides, where's the enjoyment in life if I can't relish the thought of coming back to haunt you?"

Sonya announced that she was going to bed. She still had lots of preparing to do for our little murder scene the following night. "Francesca, you know where everyone's beds are. Only one of you has to take the couch, which opens up, by the way, and I left blankets ..."

"Go, go on to bed, Sonya," Fran interrupted her. "I know where everything is. Besides, I think most of us won't be far behind you."

"I'm pretty tired too. I think I'll go up now." said Gilles, "Isabelle, you should tell these guys about your grandmother Bella's claim to fame and how she paraded it in her long velour gowns at church."

Gilles bounced up the steps and disappeared behind Sonya. I frowned for a second. I was certain I'd glimpsed a mischievous grin on his face.

Francesca was right about how tired everyone was. Everyone, that is, except Craig. Calum had volunteered for the couch and, much to his dismay, Craig decided that this was an opportune time to find out more about the company he was auditing.

I said that I was headed up too and asked Francesca if she was coming.

"Wait, Isabelle, I can help you with your bags." Calum was on his feet.

"No, no, don't bother, you guys stay," said Francesca, "I can carry Isabelle's other suitcase."

Francesca reminded Craig not to stay up too late because Poppy would be awake early.

"Night, guys." I climbed the stairs with Francesca close behind.

"So?" Of course she wasn't about to forget the kiss she'd witnessed earlier.

"No, there is no 'so'. We're just friends who happened to get a little carried away. The country air caught us by surprise, that's all." We were at the top of the stairs and Francesca was opening a door to what I assumed was my bedroom.

"Country air, my ass. Just so you know, you're gonna be breathing some country air for at least another day or two."

"I'm totally serious, Francesca, there is absolutely nothing going on, at least not like you think. So we're a tiny bit attracted, but we're not going to do anything about it — Cal knows where I stand."

"Yep, he sure looked like he knew where you were standing when I opened the door earlier. There are some extra blankets in the closet. By the way, have you noticed that when you're not being entirely honest, you talk in superlatives?"

"And this, coming from the Queen of Superlatives herself."

"If I were you, I'd come up with a better excuse than country air before Tony comes home. Don't get me wrong, I think Calum is a definite improvement over Tony but ..."

"Francesca, you need your sleep. Besides, I won't have to explain anything to Tony, because Cal is wrapping up his audit next week and he'll be gone to Montreal by the time Tony comes home."

"Hmm, I wouldn't be so sure about that if I were you ..."

"Francesca, you have an overactive imagination. Now, give me a hug, woman, and get yourself to bed."

I stood and watched her walk away. Her door closing coincided with another door opening. Gilles looked at me with a question in his eyes.

"Isabelle, do you want to hear about my parents' love letters during the war?" This was a rather odd question. I responded with a blank look. "I think I mentioned in that note I left that I had found something in the attic that might help you with the hooked rug."

Any trace of sleepiness disappeared instantly. "Yes," I said eagerly. "Come in here so we don't disturb anyone."

Gilles was in my room for less than a half hour, but he left me with more questions not less.

Gilles said the letters between his parents were filled with intimacy and hope for their future together after the war. And as awful as he had been, Gilles' father had deliberately left those letters for his son to discover. It was bittersweet that he couldn't bear to live with his son's forgiveness for the past, but knew deep down that the letters and his death would someday free his future.

When Gilles finally explained the contents of the one letter that warned Gilles' mother to stay away from my grandmother, I was intrigued. The reference to my grandmother and the hooked rug was not as conclusive as I would have wanted. Still, it did give me hope that somehow I would trace its origins back to her.

According to Gilles' father, my grandmother had fancy ideas that could infect his fiancée if she befriended her. He wrote that my grandmother had wanted hooked rugs to represent the Stations of the Cross in the church. Imagine that, hooked rugs of half-naked people! She also had another quirk that confirmed she should be avoided. Apparently she forced spring bulbs to bloom all year long. According to Gilles' father this simply wasn't natural.

I stood there thinking of the love letters Gilles' parents had exchanged. I hoped I could read them some day. It was hard for me to imagine his father writing a sweet *billet doux* to his fiancée. I remembered him as a dark and impenetrable alcoholic with a mean temper. No one including Gilles and his siblings understood why his mother had put up with him all those years.

I undressed quickly and slipped under the blankets, but it was cold and when I thought of ways to warm up, only one name and one body filled my mind but as I had learned long ago, ghosts from the past do nothing to keep you warm. So I just kept shivering until the blankets lured me to sleep.

•          •          •

She was there again, the faceless woman in the mirror, still working arduously at the frame though it looked like she was in a millinery of some sort. It wasn't one of the fashionable types of hat shops like those you might find today on Spring Garden Road.

This place was more like a garment factory. A little boy was standing next to her, perhaps a son. It was the kind of day that the little one would likely grow up forgetting about in the blur of his childhood.

Throughout the dream, I tried to concentrate so that I could make out the woman's face. Slowly her features began appearing in an unfocused blur. First I could make out a rather thin sad mouth that had an ambiguous smile. And though she seemed to be working very hard, there were no furrows on her brow. Her skin was still youthful, lily white and firm. Only her eyes were still obscured.

I had an indefinable feeling that her eyes held something of significance for me to see. At first I couldn't get over the certainty that she was secretly happy. But then I was engulfed with sadness: this was a woman who would remain nameless and faceless because, her husband wasn't a king, except perhaps, in the eyes of his wife.

Friday, October 30th 2000

*Chère* Terry,

You managed to progress from giving me a smile to making me laugh out loud. No, I don't look like Juliette Binoche, as you can see from the attached pic.

Now, about that innocent comment of yours re. my being first at breaking the chain letter — sounds vaguely like a challenge? I happen to be incapable of resisting anything remotely sounding like a challenge, so prepare to be the first to break the chain. Even the scary warning about your expired security certificate couldn't deter me now. That just reminded me of a line from *The Princess Bride*, "Prepare to die". Have you seen it? Sort of a cross between *Alice in Wonderland* and *Le Petit Prince*, less *extraordinaire* but still very entertaining.

Last Saturday, I went to the market with my hooked rug in search of the woman Sonya had told me about. No luck. However, I met this new photographer from Australia who had the coolest photographs of what he called "his jewel". The natural scenery in his photos was lush and vivid. I saw no sterile or monotonous architecture, just the architecture of God(?) The shadows had such meaning. By contrast, our modern architecture reduces us to colourless, insubstantial shadows. When I'm paranoid, I think there's a plot to build huge concrete blocks made of smaller concrete cells, like ant cells, so we'll feel small and vulnerable. By behaving like our misconception of ants, we lose power to evoke our own history & environment. We rely on the generosity of those who may feed us or crush us at whim. (That's the shortest version of my Acadian heritage, by the way, except that those who have stayed in the villages are still nearest God's architecture!)

The Farmer's Market in Halifax is a glowing exception to this. I love to be there amid the flurry of conversations around me. I like to try to read the softness in people's eyes and watch the way they move around each other.

Back to the photographer. The surprise came when he took one look at the inscription on my rug and proposed that we go to his studio and take pictures of it (I think he used extra long exposure and/or infrared film). Anyway, there it was: "Manouche". That's the inscription! I never heard it before, so it can't be Acadian and it wasn't in my dictionary, either. Now, if I could only see the model's eyes ...

Hope my jpeg attachment will lay to rest all axe murderer talk! Enjoy your visitors — I'm out in the country right now at my friend Sonya's house in Lunenburg for An Evening of Murder that will happen on all Hallow's Eve — will look forward to your photo!!

*Gros Bisou*,
Isabelle

Lost in the countryside, October 2000

*Chère* Terry,

Hey this should earn me bonus points in our little challenge: two messages in a row … but I had to share this with you. Remember how I told you that since I started working on *Smoke Damage* I've had this feeling that someone is trying to pull me into another century? Well, yesterday when I was looking for a costume for the murder mystery I had a vision of that same woman from my dreams. Then last night she reappeared. This time with a young boy. She was still sitting at a frame, hooking a rug.

Maybe this little mystery is playing with my sanity. Either that, or my life is so bland lately that I'm making up for it in my imagination.

Last night, when I was driving to Sonya's place in the country with Calum, I fell asleep and dreamt about another foggy night a long time ago when my parents picked up John and me from the train station. In one of the short stories John wrote about our romance, he captured my parents' banter so well. He described how "the fog descended like a whale in dark water and swallowed us whole." It was hard to discern more than five feet of white line on the road ahead when my mother, a gifted worrier, began to worry: "Oh, for God's sake, slow down. You can't see the road." My father laughed until he coughed. "Just do what I do. Close your eyes," he'd responded, laughing dementedly. We never slowed down.

It had been such a beautiful weekend. I remember telling John all these stories about Acadian history and my ancestors. I even shared a few of my own theories about the women that were never written about, but only the naughty ones. I remember how he laughed in exactly the same way as my history teacher had when I'd tried to explain the project I wanted to write. I had changed topics for the history project — I would change topics with John.

We held hands all weekend, during walks in the park, strolling by my old high school peering through the windows, and along the fly-infested *digue* by the fish plant where I discovered my father's old boat all battered and patched on the starboard side. This upset me enormously since Papa had taken such painstaking care of it when he owned it.

Then the dream shifted to another love story, albeit a sadder part of it. John had also written a story about the weeks preceding my father's death, when Mama had been trying to figure out what Dad was building in the basement. At one point, she even considered he might be building his own coffin. But Papa was a romantic even when facing his own mortality. He was in love with my mother from the moment he laid eyes on her until the very day he died …

Do you believe this kind of love still exists?

Isabelle

Paris — October 31, 2000

Happy Halloween, Isabelle!

Vision? Wait a minute! Is this the first time this has happened? You mention it so casually and without giving me any details!! I am becoming more and more bewitched. Now, about our chain letter, here's a little quote to inspire you:

"The time has come, the walrus said
To speak of many things
Of shoes and ships and sealing wax
Of cabbages and kings
And why the sea is boiling hot
And whether pigs have wings …"

You'll recognize the Lewis Carroll quote, I'm sure. I believe the time has come to formalize this contest. Shall we set forty-eight hours as the limit for response time, barring exploding laptops and death? To provide a weekly break I suggest the twenty-four hours of Sunday be held in abeyance. In addition, at least once a week we must tell an event from our past (touching, funny, intriguing, salacious, frivolous and/or spontaneous) that has burrowed into our brains. I would suggest a wager but my mind is rather gutter-ridden. Oh, and by the way, there are no bonus points!

Meanwhile I think I can be of some assistance in the riddle of your hooked rug … Your inscription, "Manouche" — I am surprised that you didn't recognize it immediately given your love of gypsy music. A Manouche is a French gypsy. Any chance you'll change your name? Not that Isabelle isn't a lovely name, but somehow Manouche seems to suit you. I can say that with certainty now that I have your photograph. I hope you won't mind, but I took the liberty of framing it. It sits here next to my computer so that when I write to you, you are smiling in my direction. You are really quite stunning, Isabelle, and your eyes remind me of the ocean.

In addition to his many other attributes, it appears that John was also a talented writer. I wonder whether Tony or his brother Calum has any hopes of living up to that memory. You see I have my own psychic abilities. It is clear to me that this Calum has the hots for you.

I assume you must have noticed by now. It's a rather dysfunctional little trio though, don't you think? Isabelle, do you think anyone can ever live up to your memories of John?

I would like to hear more stories about your past, including your parents. Why not include some excerpts from that story you mention? Since I'm not threatened by this John, a story of true love could go a long way to restore my faith in that possibility. My life is barren when it comes to any new possibilities.

Enjoy the rest of your murderous weekend and write soon,

Terry

# Chapter 9
## Setting the Stage for a Murder

After the drive through the fog the night before, the morning's sun peeking through the curtains was a welcome tickle to my nose. Soon the aroma of brewing coffee replaced all of the sun's relevance. I headed downstairs and found Calum and Gilles sitting at Sonya's kitchen table chopping vegetables and chatting up a storm. One could have mistaken them for long-lost pals. What a strange duo they made.

"Good morning, Sunshine, are we in a good mood today or are we feeling a bit catty, by any chance?"

Calum got up as he spoke and came over to kiss me on the forehead. His eyes lingered on my black kimono sporting colourful tropical birds all over it. Yep, Erotica was awake. "Uhmm, you smell delicious," he whispered, and added out loud, "Want some espresso? We made it extra strong, just the way you like it."

"I take it Gilles has been filling you in on my family namesake?" I reached inside the cupboard, pausing momentarily to pick out a suitably unique pottery mug.

"Here you go." Calum poured the aromatic tar into my cup.

"Thanks, uhmmm, this smells like heaven. So you think my being a *Piquine* is amusing, do you?"

*Piquine* was the nickname given to everybody in the family, including extended relatives on my grandmother Bella's side. Referring to our catty nature, it recognized our appreciation for creature comforts, and revealed us to be alternately aloof, arrogant, proud and playful, not to mention apt to sharpen our claws upon unsuspecting victims when we were adequately provoked.

"Rather appropriate, I'd say," Craig added as he strolled in. He stopped in front of the ceiling fan that hovered in the middle of the kitchen and began swatting at the string, much as a cat would have done with a dangling piece of yarn. "Meow."

"Where are the girls? And where is my little pumpkin, Poppy?" I glanced at the clock. It was barely nine o'clock.

"Francesca and Sonya just went outside with Poppy to decorate the yard for tonight. They left us men in charge of the food preparation. Wouldn't you say that's a radical and welcome change from the good old Chéticamp tradition of women only in the kitchen?"

I could hardly get over the transformation in Gilles since I'd met him again a month before. Maybe I'd been altogether mistaken about how awkward he was. Or was it plausible that, like me, he reverted to an outdated and neurotic version of himself whenever he ran into people from Chéticamp? If that were the case, I should have felt flattered that he seemed relatively at ease, even normal (whatever that was) with my friends.

"Well, I'm going to go find those three." With mug in hand, I headed into the porch that led to the back door.

"Hey, wait a second, shouldn't you get dressed? You're gonna freeze out there." Calum caught me by the waist from behind. "Or are you planning to drive me crazy all morning with that sexy kimono?" He was talking into my ear and kissing my neck at the same time.

"Don't you have vegetables to chop or something?" I squirmed loose and went outside. I heard another meow just before the door slammed behind me.

As I hopped down the steps and was sauntering along the cool grass, I was surprised to come face to face with a stranger.

"Hey, Isabelle, sorry if I startled you."

"Philippe, what the hell are you doing here?" But we were interrupted.

"Isabelle, is that you back there?" Sonya came around the corner of the house. "So, you've been reacquainted with Philippe. Did he tell you Gilles invited him and that he's got a character for tonight's murder mystery?"

"No, we just bumped into each other when you showed up." I was more than a little confused by this turn of events. "Okay, is someone going to give me some details here?"

"Why don't you two come and check out the front yard and I'll fill you in on the way." Sonya was pulling me away with a newfound liveliness.

"Actually, I have to get back to the cottage or the coffee pot will burn a hole in the stove, but I will leave Sonya here to fill you in. Bella, we've certainly got a lot of catching up to do. Before I run back, though, you should know that ..." But Philippe's voice trailed off. "Oh, never mind, the rest can wait for later. But here, give me a hug."

We shared a longish hug as I looked over his shoulder in Sonya's direction. I was speechless in my bewilderment.

I looked back to see Philippe disappear towards a smallish cottage on the other side of the fence. He still had that Richard Gere look, greying but handsome.

"Okay, so what's the scoop? I can't believe that Philippe is going to be playing this game tonight and no one thought to mention it to me." I paused for a moment.

"Sonya, is it just me or do you also think it is more than an extraordinary coincidence that I am playing An Evening of Murder tonight with two of my former neighbours from Chéticamp? Not to mention that, until recently, I hadn't seen either of them in more than twenty years."

"Oh, it's weird all right. Judging by my visit there this morning, I'm beginning to wonder whether the Bermuda Triangle has moved north."

Rounding the corner, we found Francesca busy propping up some fake tombstones all over the yard while Poppy concentrated intently on one of the pumpkins on the veranda.

"Hey, what's all this?" I said. Sonya certainly didn't believe in going halfway. "Hi, Poppy, how is my little pumpkin doing?" I picked up Poppy, who greeted me with one of her fat adorable grins.

"Oh, Isabelle, thank God you're up. You're never going to believe who I met this morning. None other than Philippe Langlois." Francesca turned to Poppy, "Hey, my little squirt, aren't you tickled pink with all this attention you're getting."

"Yes," I said, "Philippe, yeah, I sort of just met him."

"And?"

"And what?" I looked at Francesca rather blankly for a moment and then all the pieces fell into place.

"Holy shit, the Armani suit! I was positive I remembered him from somewhere. But, Francesca, just wait till you hear this. Philippe lived next door to me in Chéticamp for about two years when I was a kid. I knew I recognized him from somewhere, but it's no wonder. The only clothes I ever saw Philippe wearing were faded khakis and T-shirts."

"This is positively bizarre. Do you think Gilles recognized him that day?"

"No, I'm sure he didn't or he would've said something. I still can't believe that he's playing this Evening of Murder with us tonight."

"Yeah, when Francesca told me about that newspaper incident and how Philippe showed up at Craig's parents', I thought it was pretty whacked too, and now it's gotten even wackier." Every now and again, Sonya had a way of articulating exactly how things were.

"I just hope they don't start talking about that newspaper incident again." I turned to Francesca. "Weren't you saying how furious he was when you saw him that day?"

"Actually he seemed really laid back about the whole thing this morning when we were over there. His girlfriend didn't even know anything about it."

"Can you believe this crazy story, Poppy?" I said, chewing on Poppy's neck. Poppy giggled with delight. "Oh yeah, and by the way that wasn't his girlfriend but his wife, her name is Lise."

Sonya looked at me with a pained expression. "Isabelle, there's no easy way for me to say this. Gilles told me that his wife died of breast cancer a little over five years ago. I'm sorry."

"Oh, my God, poor Philippe. He must've been devastated. They were so in love."

"Hey, out there," Calum called, "we have omelettes for sale in the kitchen, anyone hungry?"

On our way in, Sonya brought me up to speed on Philippe's invitation. Maybe Gilles had recognized him.

Francesca piped in. "He's quite nice and can you believe he went back to university in his forties and just graduated from law school. His girlfriend Maria seems more of a cold fish, though."

"Yeah, she's rather snobby." That was a strong statement coming from Sonya, who always seemed to see the good side in everyone.

"So, who's this oddball we're talking about?" Craig was on cue. "Since when are there any nice lawyers around? Isn't that an oxymoron or something?"

"Gilles, what's this I hear about you inviting Philippe tonight? And, how come you never said anything that day we were at Timothy's?"

"I didn't recognize Philippe that day either. He's the one who recognized me on the bus last week." Gilles said that he never got to know them. They were sort of New Age tree-hugging types and kind of reclusive, he thought. The rumour going round was that she was a pot head and that the drug dealers in town assumed wrong when they figured Philippe would go easy on them.

Gilles explained that he ran into Philippe the same day he had talked to Sonya on the phone. She was thinking of calling it off because someone else couldn't make it. Gilles and Philippe got to talking about Chéticamp and how Gilles had run into me.

"Anyway, I told him about tonight and he seemed genuinely interested so I called Sonya back."

"I can hardly believe he's a lawyer and that Lise died of cancer."

I had thought they were the coolest couple I'd ever met. I didn't know anything about drugs. I did remember how nice they were. They used to take me along on hikes and we would collect plants and flowers and then frame them. Philippe showed me how to take photographs in the moonlight using a tripod. They ate different foods like fondue, and when they made Chinese food we'd eat on cushions on the floor and use chopsticks. They had the coolest furniture, too.

Gilles was surprised that my parents let me hang out there. He assumed that most of the older people in Chéticamp thought Philippe and Lise were dangerous hippies. But, my parents loved them. We would have potluck dinners with them all the time and play board games. Back then Philippe was interested in the decrease of cod stocks. He and my father used to discuss the impending collapse of the East Coast fishery long before the problem was even defined by our senile politicians.

Over breakfast Sonya told us that Philippe's girlfriend was what's called a protocol person, someone who sets up temporary offices for visiting politicians and dignitaries and arranged the formal and schmoozing events they attended.

It was hard for me to imagine Philippe with someone like that. Lise was perhaps the most laid-back and informal person I'd ever met. I never had to worry about things like tracking dirt in their house or dropping crumbs or even combing my hair.

The other great thing about Lise was that she was always home after school. She used to bake those weird-tasting cookies, the nutritious kind. I would hang out with her until Mam got home from work. Lise was always interested in what we'd done at school and she would help me with my homework.

"Uhmm-hmm, this tastes awesome, what kind of cheese is this, it sure packs a mean bite?" Francesca asked. She had lost interest in Philippe.

I remembered that I hadn't said anything about my dream yet. "Hey, I was going to tell you guys that I had a dream last night that solved all my problems with these two characters I'll be playing in a couple of weeks."

"I think it's called *Piquine* cheese ... Isabelle should like it?" Calum had been very quiet but now as he spoke, he stretched his foot under the table and started grazing his way up my leg.

"You know you're not ingratiating yourself with any of these catty comments." With that, I delivered one swift kick under the table. "If you're not careful, you'll end up on the same shit list Craig's on right now."

"Hey, what'd I do?"

I ignored Craig's question and told them about the dream and how it had solved my problem. I would make the Tart the reincarnation of Rebecca. "At least something productive came out of Craig's badgering last night."

"What kinda stupid name is that, Tart?"

"Craig, could you concentrate on not having Poppy look like a bunch of mashed carrots by the time you finish feeding her." As she spoke, Francesca got up and went over to wipe Poppy's face. I wondered if I could ever transform into such a doting mother. Probably not.

"No, I'm serious. How many people have you met before with the name Tart?"

"Well, how many people have you met with the name Poppy? Does that make it a stupid name too?"

Sonya intervened. "All right, you two, no couple spats in my kitchen. Besides, before I forget, I have a terribly belated birthday present for Isabelle. I realize I'm almost two months late, but it took me a while to finish it." Sonya was getting a giftwrapped present from the cupboard. She handed it to me.

"What is it?" I asked eagerly. "Not another severed finger, I hope?"

"Just open it."

As I tore into the wrapping paper with the excitement of a little kid, Francesca was looking at Calum looking at me. She told me later that it was at that moment she was sure he was falling for me. And as much as Francesca couldn't stand Tony, she wasn't so sure that his brother was all that different underneath his well-polished exterior.

"Oh, Sonya, it's divine. I love it." I jumped up and gave Sonya a hug. "But, how did you know?"

"Happy birthday! Francesca told me about all that funky underwear I missed at your birthday party. Sorry it's so late."

It was a painting of a clothesline. "First the shower curtain and now this. You guys are too much. I can't wait to get home now so I can hang it up."

Francesca turned to Gilles and Calum, who were exchanging quizzical glances.

"This past summer when Isabelle was back in Chéticamp, she was obsessed with her neighbour's clothesline. She kept having these crazy fantasies of floating and dancing inside the clothes. Anyway, when she got back in September we threw her a birthday party, got out our funkiest underwear and hung them up on a clothesline in my living room. I even found this unique shower curtain. You might have noticed it in her bathroom, Calum? It has colourful clothing hanging on rows of clotheslines."

"Yeah, the only thing we didn't recreate was that other little fixation of hers — the black bra against a fiery red sunset." Naturally Craig wasn't going to let this opportunity pass him by.

"Now that sounds interesting. Do tell ..." said Calum.

"She thought she would scandalize the locals by displaying a lacy black bra on a small clothesline hanging on the front veranda and then set up a camera to take pictures of it against the sunset."

"Craig, you make it sound like I was deliberately trying to be obscene."

"Weren't you?"

"I'll say," said Calum, "more like provocative or erotic if you ask me. Not that I mean that in a bad way." He winked at me. From the look on her face, Francesca was feeling more than a little nauseated.

"You two are pathetic. It was a statement about how the artistic spirit can be suppressed by religious dogma. Gilles can relate to it. I was thinking that I would superimpose an image of the church steeple in the background."

"Well, I don't care how you try to pass it off, I still say your primary goal was scandalizing the neighbours ..." Even as he said it, Craig knew he was stepping over the line.

I got up and headed towards the living room. Gilles followed me and said he thought it would make a great image. He thought he might even take a stab at painting it.

I figured he'd like the idea. I told him I was going to put my painting in a safe place so it wouldn't be caught in the crossfire of murderers later that evening.

As I was going up the stairs, Sonya caught up with me. She said she hoped the painting would remind me of the side of me that wasn't hidden or faceless but beautiful.

"Francesca was telling me about your series of faceless women and wondering about its symbolism. She seemed worried that you were taking the whole subconscious thing too seriously. Here." She handed me a card.

I opened it and read:

Dear Isabelle,

Not only are you creative and free-spirited but you have a tremendously compassionate nature when the occasion calls for it. If that's what your past has given you, then you should celebrate it rather than let it haunt you. I am very happy that we are becoming closer friends and hope we will share many more birthdays together.

With much affection,
Sonya.

I gave Sonya a warm hug. She had single-handedly turned my day around.

I pointed to an old photograph enlargement hanging on Sonya's wall. "Who is that?" I asked. "Every time I come up the stairs I feel him staring at me."

"Oh, that's Mr. Conrad. He's kind of my own little piece of guesswork, like your rug. I found him this summer while I was renovating the co-op. He was sandwiched behind a brick wall in the basement." Sonya rented out a room in a Halifax co-op so she didn't have to commute all winter on icy roads. She used the house in Lunenburg from spring to late fall and on most weekends after that.

"What's his story?"

"I don't know. I haven't had time to do any research yet."

"Don't you think it's funny that we both found mysterious characters from the past this summer?" Without waiting for an answer I gave Sonya a last quick hug, bolted upstairs into my room and shut the door behind me.

I had just opened my suitcase when there was a knock at the door.

"Yeah?"

"Isabelle, can I talk to you?" But rather than wait for a response, Calum opened the door, came inside and shut the door behind him.

"Cal, I'm not in the mood, I just want to get dressed so I can help Sonya decorate."

"I know, I know, so do I, but I was out-of-line downstairs and I want to apologize. I didn't think you'd get upset, you know we were just teasing."

"Forget it."

"No, I can't just forget it 'cause I know you're pissed. How do you think I can have fun tonight knowing you're upset with me?"

"Look, if it makes you feel any better I'm not really pissed. I think I'm just going through some kind of crisis that has nothing to do with you or Craig. Besides, you and I both know that we're not about to start anything …"

"What? Is it Tony?"

"No, Cal, this has nothing to do with Tony. There, does that make you happy? It's another one of those moot points, isn't it?"

"No, it isn't a moot point. But what about the other night? Tony said he loved you? What about that? Are you saying there was nothing to it?"

"Tony was drunk and acting out. That's all."

"But doesn't that tell you something? He must have feelings for you or he wouldn't have been acting out, would he?"

"Look, for whatever it's worth, there is nothing remotely romantic between Tony and me, nor is there any possibility for anything in the future. Now, can I get dressed?" I wasn't sure if I was trying to convince Calum or myself.

"In other words, if Tony is not standing between us, there's no reason for me to back off, is there?" Again, I had a hunch that Calum was testing me.

"Cal, I don't want to hear this. Can't we just agree to be friends and forget all about this morning?"

"I don't know. Can we?"

"But Cal …"

"No, there's no buts allowed in this conversation. I do want you as a friend. But, I might also want more than that. All I know is that I don't think I've ever met anyone like you before and I'm not willing to let you talk me out of my feelings. There, how's that for honesty?" It *was* a test. He was lying.

"I think there was a but in that little speech." I turned back to my suitcase hoping to hide my expression. It was starting to look like I might have to lock up Erotica in one of the cupboards for the rest of the weekend. As much as I wanted to sabotage any chances with Tony something was holding me back.

"What I think is that you two are so in love that neither of you will ever seriously consider a relationship with anyone else. If you ask me, both of you need to let go of the past."

"That's ridiculous."

"Whatever, will you at least consider the possibility that I am not a complete asshole?"

"Maybe."

"I guess that's something to go on. Think we could seal it with a kiss?" He laughed because he knew my answer.

As he left, I had a sinking feeling. Did I need to let go of the past? Was it by letting go of history that we might become who we will be?

The rest of the day was taken up in a flurry of preparations for the main event. Gilles, Sonya and I devoted ourselves to covering the furniture with white sheets and placing fake cobwebs, motheaten curtains, and gothic candelabras in strategic spots. Since the murder mystery game was supposed to be set in an abandoned old mansion, we decided to move the kitchen table to the living room, where a fire could be lit in the fireplace for added atmosphere.

It was also during this time that I became increasingly aware of a certain attraction developing between Gilles and Sonya. I had been so preoccupied that I had somehow missed something very real going on there. It should have occurred to me as a possibility before. Both loved the arts. Was it mutual or did most of the interest stem from Gilles?

Perhaps this explained the new side of Gilles I was seeing. Whatever the cause, it certainly suited him. Of all of us, he seemed the most excited about the haunted house séance. Sonya was playing the role of the gracious hostess, but whether or not she was genuinely interested in Gilles as more than a friend was hard to detect.

The hours passed quickly and before I knew it, I was back in my room transforming into a world-renowned psychic. I had brought my tarot cards and crystal ball as props and was borrowing some of Sonya's clothing to complete my character's look.

I held the crystal ball up against the fading light of the window. It was the one that John had bought me at the circus. Some days it seemed like a lifetime ago. Held against this filtering light, the crystal seemed to play a trick on my sense of time. When my eyes began filling up, I told myself it must have been the glare.

I dropped the crystal ball in my pocket and rushed over to my laptop to send another quick note to Terry. Once I had pressed the [Send] key, I turned my attention to the handbook that came with the game.

An Evening of Murder included a character manual for each guest that no one was supposed to open before they are instructed by the hostess to do so. However, I had hosted these murder mysteries before. Between my persuasive sales pitch and my penchant for theatrical effects, I had convinced Sonya to let me bring the manual with me to prepare a dramatic entrance.

I took one last look in the mirror, adjusted the scarves in my haphazardly upswept 'do and gave a little nudge to the huge hoop earrings so that they would jingle as I walked.

"Let the games begin," I said as I prepared to descend.

All Hallow's Eve, 2000

Dear Terry,

I am replying well within the allotted timeframe. I can't believe that Manouche refers to a French gypsy. Inconceivable! Now I am all the more intrigued by this hooked rug. As soon as I get back to the city, I am going to delve into this mystery once and for all. No more floundering. I must find out who made it and what's the story behind it!!

"O oysters, come and walk with us!" The walrus did beseech. "A pleasant walk, a pleasant talk, Along the briny beach."

Thanks for the trip down memory lane with the quote from Alice's *Through the Looking Glass*. A wager, hmmm ... well, since I know this will either end in a declaration of stalemate or in my being declared victor, I am tempted to go for the big one — How about a trip to Paris? I will think about it some more though, but now for the story part:

I only have a few minutes before descending to the big dinner (naturally, I must keep them waiting a bit), but I thought I might start telling you about the love story of my parents. It is, after all, the only one I know that lasted a lifetime.

They were first introduced during the winter of '42, a couple of Acadians from neighbouring French communities. He asked her to a dance and the next day confessed to a fellow lumberjack, "I've just met the girl I am going to marry."

He was a handsome man then, strong from his labours — cutting timber in the winter, hauling lobster traps in the summer. He need not have worked so hard. He made enough at either job to support himself. But he was proud, a man of substance and dignity. The Bible says a man must work by the sweat on his brow, and he was nothing if not a good Christian.

One day, in her presence, he lifted a fifty-pound weight with his little finger. His friends on the dock shook their heads and smiled wryly.

It was quite a feat. And she laughed gaily, overjoyed at his efforts to impress her. That was 1942. (To be continued)

That's all for now — I'm beckoned to a murder scene. Hope it will remain a game, though there could be some strange tensions in the air, to say the least. I think I told you about the guy whose newspaper was stolen a while back in a café. Turns out he was an old neighbour of mine when I was a young kid. Now he's been invited to play with us tonight. And then there's Francesca, who appears to have developed an intense dislike for Calum although she's pretending otherwise. She's very protective of me when it comes to men, but I think she should know by now that I'm a big girl who can take care of herself.

*Je t'embrasse*
— Isabelle (a.k.a. Manouche!)

Paris, November 1

Dear Manouche!

If my opinion counts for anything, I don't think this Calum guy deserves you either. Sounds like Francesca is perceptive in her distrust of these brothers. I like Francesca already. Don't be too hard on her if she seems overprotective, she's obviously just looking out for you.

Sometimes, that's one aspect of being in Paris that's rather lonely. Most of my friends are in Québec and the people I hang out with here are mostly academics. Of course, they're very friendly, but we usually end up talking about university. At least I've made two great friends in the last year, Dédier, my pal in Brittany and you, of course.

I think you're lucky to have parents who were so in love. Mine always seemed to be fighting. Hope you'll continue with their love story. You're making me a believer. Meantime, I guess I owe you a story. I'm afraid I'm not as creative as you and my life hasn't been all that exciting. Still, I had pretty good times in Montreal during my undergraduate studies:

One night I was gathered with a bunch of friends. We were all struggling to make ends meet when my girlfriend came up with an idea. You would've liked Geneviève, she was intelligent and passionate. She used to wear a black velvet smoking jacket that matched her velvety voice perfectly. She also sang in a jazz group on weekends and I was insanely jealous of all the men who would come on to her. In the end, my jealousy drove her away. Geneviève was perhaps the closest I've come to knowing true love. After we broke up, I had reckless relationships with reckless women and consider myself lucky I came out of it with nothing more than cynicism. That's when I became more of a loner and really embraced academia. Underneath it all, though, I've always wanted love, just not the kind I know. I guess I'd like to find my soulmate, though I'm skeptical such a thing exists.

Sorry, I veered off topic. The story. Well, Geneviève came up with the idea that our group could lease a warehouse from her father and convert it into loft spaces. In exchange for building them we could have free rent and then, when we graduated, her father could rent them out for ten times what they were worth at the time. It was a great idea and we all ended up living like kings during our undergrad years. We even came up with a way of making money out of it. We finished one entire storey during first year and decided to sublet that space to other students while we worked our way up and built more lofts. By our last year, we were raking in some serious cash, at least for university students. Nowadays, the same lofts we built are considered prime real estate in Montreal. I ended up buying one real cheap. I sublet it before coming to Paris and it gives me some added cash to play with while I'm in here.

I guess it's not really a mind-blowing story. I just thought about telling you last night after I saw this Cuban movie called *The Waiting List*. I really liked the part that reminded me of our loft-building days. You should see it. Now I have to get to work. You have forty-eight hours to respond. The clock is ticking.

Love,
Terry

## Chapter 10
### Ghosts, Goblins and Other Spectres

"Where is Isabelle, anyway?" It was Calum's turn to introduce his character.

"Were you, by any chance, asking about me? And the name is not Isabelle, it's Isabella, your psychic channeller for this evening's *séance*." As I swept down the staircase, I stopped abruptly and gasped in front of a body lying on the floor. The handle of a butcher's knife stuck out from its chest and fake blood had oozed onto the floor.

"Heaven and earth shiver my timbers! Oh, can I ever sense the vibes of murderous secrecy and evil here." As I made my way towards the dining table, I brushed the light switch, leaving the room in darkness except for the candles and the fire in the fireplace. The rest of the players responded with an appropriate "Ah" of shock. "Oh, yes, there are definitely dark forces at work in this room."

"Who are you, anyway?" I said to Calum, but before he could answer I continued, "No, wait; don't speak, don't speak — I feel an aura about you. You are a very popular personality, are you not? I think you are somehow connected with radios, but you are very devious, a seedy character, dare I say? Correct me if I'm wrong."

"Well, not that I believe in this psycho-mumbo-jumbo, but on this you were informed correctly. I am Carlos Stern, otherwise known as the 'shock jock' of the waves." Calum was reeking with arrogance as he spoke. Francesca looked pleased. This might be a welcome change from Calum's overly-polished persona.

Francesca got up with a Camcorder and approached me. "Finally someone with an interesting slant for my readers. Isabella, what other juicy predictions do you have about the people in this room?"

"Get that thing out of my face, it interferes with the spirits trying to communicate with me. Besides, I have nothing to say that would belong in your scandalous rag. You are the filthy editor of that piece of trash, are you not?"

"Just because I believe the public has a right to information, that doesn't make me a criminal. You know what they say: where there's smoke, there's fire. I take offence to your slanderous accusation. Judge Gillespie, do you think I'd have a case for slander?" She addressed her question to Gilles, who was dressed in judgelike attire right down to the gavel he began rapping fervently on the dining table.

"I believe we are gathered here for a *séance* and not the preamble for a hearing on slander," he said. "I refuse to listen to this stupidity. Now, Isabella, I suggest you take a seat so we can get this ridiculous *séance* over with."

"Not that I take orders from anyone other than my spiritual muses, but I do see a gorgeous young man over there whose aura I wouldn't mind getting in touch with. And, Judge Gillespie, I suggest you stop banging that silly gavel of yours unless you are determined to scare away all of our spiritual messengers." I walked over to the other side of the table and made everyone move so that I could sit beside Philippe. "Uhm, and who might you be, you handsome devil? And is that an Armani suit, you're sporting?" I flashed a knowing wink in Francesca's direction.

Although he was supposed to be playing the part of a sexy photographer, Philippe's blush was visible, even in the candlelight. "Uh, hi, I'm Attila. I just got back from Bermuda, where we were shooting next season's bathing suit edition."

"And who's that over there, your cover model?" I pointed my long fake fingernails at the only woman I didn't know. "Although, if she doesn't stop hogging the antipasto platter, she won't exactly fit the image of a model bathing suit babe, now will she? The least she could do is share."

Maria, Philippe's girlfriend, having been caught red-handed, passed the platter over rather ungraciously. Judging by the look in her eye, I gathered that she was a tad territorial about her man. This only fuelled Isabella's ebullient performance.

*Erotica, this is our night*, I thought to myself.

"Now ladies, no need to start a food fight, there's plenty more to come." Sonya spoke as she emerged from the kitchen, decked out in her apron and chef's hat. She was carrying a large black tray with rows of crostini topped with smoked salmon or prosciutto, artfully displayed so that the white bread on black china looked suspiciously like a skeleton.

"Why, Isabella, I am delighted that you were finally able to join us. I'm your hostess extraordinaire, and I will be serving your delicacies tonight. I trust you've met everyone. And, as long as you don't mind my occasional trips to the kitchen, I think this séance you have planned for us should begin."

"I haven't had the pleasure of introducing myself to Isabella. The name's Charles Craigmore ..." said Craig, who had finally decided to join the cast, "and I don't need any *séance* to convince me that Marianna, that so-called model over there, is obviously the one who killed our beloved friend in one of her fits of jealous rage. Everyone in the business knows how spoiled rotten she is and how she retaliates mercilessly if anyone rejects her."

"That's simply not true. I loved Jack. I just don't choose to flaunt my emotional pain in public. However, I will agree with you on one count. I don't believe for one minute that we need a cheap séance led by a shoddy crystal-gazing witch to find out who Jack's killer is. Does anybody here know how much Isabella charges for one of her sessions? Talk about criminal instincts ..."

Was any of this tirade inspired by her character manual? Or was Maria throwing in a diversion to put me on the defensive to interrupt my outrageous flirting with Philippe?

For the next couple of hours, with a few respites when food was served, the accusations flew back and forth. Sonya had chosen an exceptional cast. We all stayed in character even during food breaks. Once the murderer was unveiled, we all found it awkward to return to our own personalities.

We were lounging by the fire, each with nightcap in hand and reminiscing about the evening, when the topic of Joe, the man who had swiped Philippe's newspaper, came up.

"Well, I for one, think Halifax should do something about homeless bums." Apparently Maria did not let compassion cloud her judgement.

"What would you suggest the city do," I held back from asking some of the less savoury questions going through my mind at that moment.

"Enforce a bylaw that would keep them off the streets and insist they live on welfare like everyone else who can't get a job. Isn't that why we pay such exorbitant taxes?"

"Maria, isn't that a tad harsh?" Philippe asked. "Unless someone has a fixed address they aren't eligible for financial assistance. They're dependent on soup kitchens and the goodwill of the community."

"You and I both know that this goodwill of the community goes straight to the liquor store. Don't bother looking at me mortified with your Mother Theresa act. At least I'm not a social-worky hypocrite."

Everyone including Philippe seemed horrified. Francesca, who couldn't stand silence, broke the tension by asking Gilles if he had burned his hands recently.

"No, it's eczema. But I was about to say that the guy who took Philippe's newspaper doesn't drink at all. He's a recovering alcoholic who started drinking when his wife and children died in a house fire. He lost everything including his interest in his work. Eventually his boss didn't have enough compassion to keep him on the payroll and so he fired him."

"Oh, Gilles," said Sonya, visibly moved. "That's so sad. How do you know him?"

"We used to work together in a framing shop in Montreal."

I didn't buy his explanation for his scars. Could he have been there at the fire? Somehow, I felt there was more to it. After another rather longish silence, Gilles continued.

"Joe was my supervisor. A really nice guy, easy to work for and always supportive. He even came up with the idea for my very first art exhibit and salon. He said it could be good for business ..." Gilles seemed to disappear into his own thoughts. He excused himself to use the washroom.

Maria had retreated into an uncomfortable silence and was looking ashamed in light of Gilles' explanation.

"Well, folks," said Philippe, "it's been a really enjoyable evening, but I have some writing to do in the morning and should get some sleep. I hope you'll all come over sometime for dinner or something so I can get to know your real characters. I'm sure they're just as interesting as the roles you all played tonight."

I resisted the urge to suggest that breakfast in the morning might be fun. Part of me would have loved to see the reaction playing itself out on Maria's face. However, it was obvious that Maria was feeling chagrined enough as it was. I opted for a more charitable peace offering.

"Philippe, my parents told me that you are the descendent of a rather notorious writer of historical fiction, a detail you left out when I knew you back in Chéticamp." He nodded. "I've toyed with the idea of writing myself. I'd love to find out how your grandfather earned such a flagrant reputation. Perhaps you and Maria could meet us in town sometime and we could talk about it over dinner?"

Francesca, who'd been uncharacteristically quiet, threw me the most incredulous look. But Philippe brightened visibly.

"As a matter of fact, that's what I'll be working on tomorrow. My grandfather was working on a new book about the dispersal of the Acadians when he died, how they were caught in a struggle between Europe and North America. I've been reading these journals of John Thomas, who detailed some of the events leading up to the Deportation."

I couldn't hide my immediate enthusiasm, but Maria quickly snuffed out any possibility of dinner happening in the near future.

"Phil has forgotten that we're three weeks away from a federal election and I'll be run off my feet with the temporary constituency headquarters. It's a miracle I got tonight off. After the election, I'll need a vacation to rest up for Christmas. Maybe in the new year." In other words, she couldn't care less if she ever laid eyes on me again.

Who could blame her? I hadn't exactly spent the evening befriending her. But now I had a reason to be more generous. Realising that tonight was probably not the best time to start working my charm, I was content to send Maria off with a little diplomacy and humour.

I agreed that it was a busy time of year for everyone. *Smoke Damage* was being staged around the same time as the election. But, I added that I would love to have a look at those journals sometime. "Who knows, at our next *séance* we could bring back the spirit of one of my Acadian ancestors?"

Although she was likely suspicious of my sudden cordiality, Maria responded with guarded pleasantness. It was, after all, her job to schmooze, even with people she didn't particularly like. She forced a smile and turned to Sonya.

"Thanks so much for inviting us over, Sonya. The food was delicious and you created quite the atmosphere for this ghostly affair. You should consider catering for the protocol office. You would meet influential people who could be potential buyers for your art, too."

Philippe echoed Maria's thanks and promised to get the journals to me. He added how great it had been to see us again after all these years. With a wave, he and Maria were out the door.

Our symphony of good nights followed them. Sonya closed and locked the door. Turning around, she looked at the remaining lot of us, who returned a communal blank look. Calum was the first to speak.

"Oh, c'mon guys, she wasn't that bad."

"Wasn't that bad! What would you call it? Why would a nice guy like Philippe date such a woman?" Francesca asked, baffled. The men exchanged knowing glances. "And you, Isabelle, what was this 'We should get together for dinner sometime' bullshit? Have you lost your mind completely?"

"I just felt bad for him and, besides, I am genuinely interested in these journals. The other thing is that she reminds me a lot of my neighbour Cliff. He seems to lose all social graces the second he finds himself in a room with strangers. But despite his faults he's very generous and has helped me out more than once."

Francesca reminded me that Philippe came in a package. Was Maria worth putting up with just so I could read those journals? Couldn't I just go to the Public Archives and read them there?

"Francesca," Craig piped in, "as usual, you're being too judgmental. I think Calum's right. She wasn't that horrible. Besides, there's a lot of people in the real world who think just like she does about homeless people. I don't see you socializing with anyone on street corners."

"Why can't you just be quiet for once?"

"See, that's exactly what I mean. Anyone who doesn't agree with you makes no sense, isn't that right? Francesca — the world authority on what does and doesn't make sense. This is what I have to live with."

"But Craig, I ..."

"Oh, stuff your 'I didn't mean to say it like that' crap. You meant exactly what you said. I'm tired of listening to you and Isabelle judging everyone with your holier-than-thou attitudes. I'm going to bed." He turned on his heels and headed off in the direction of the stairs.

"See, Isabelle, I keep telling you how unreasonable he is. I can't talk to him when he gets like this." I had nothing to say. I was stunned that Craig considered me as judgmental as Francesca. I could also see both sides of their grownup version of tug-of-war.

"Gosh," said Sonya, "do you think someone should go talk to him? He seemed upset about that comment."

"What comment?" Francesca was getting irate. "Who thinks I was out of line with that comment? Tell me. Sonya, do you think I was out of line? Tell me. 'Cause if I was out of line, I want to know. As far as Craig is concerned, if a woman is the least bit attractive then she's entitled to her opinion. Well, some opinions are unacceptable."

"Sounds to me like this is more about you and Craig than it is about Maria," said Calum.

"Of course, you're going to agree with him. You're a man.

"Besides, I was asking Isabelle and Sonya. You know what I don't want any answers. It's late and I'm going to bed. Knowing Craig, he'll still be pissed off in the morning. As he would say, that's what I have to put up with." Francesca hugged Sonya and me and then followed Craig upstairs.

"What the hell did I do to deserve that?" I felt like asking Calum if it had ever occurred to him that not everything was about him. Instead I answered his question.

"Nothing, Cal, Francesca's just upset, that's all. Those two are going through growing pains and she wasn't herself all evening. I think that argument started long before any of us got involved. Let's not dwell on it. It's not that late and we've been stuffing our faces all night. I, for one, vote on going for a midnight stroll."

"You can't be serious?" Sonya wasn't used to going to bed late.

"Oh, c'mon, you lazy bums. In another month we'll be freezing our asses out there. Why not enjoy the half-decent temperature while we still can? Besides, I think there's a full moon out and it's not officially Halloween until I've howled at the moon!"

Although they all agreed that I had lost my mind, the trio decided to tag along. As we walked past Philippe's cottage, I couldn't resist peering over. All the lights were out except for a strange glow that looked like it might be coming from an oil lamp. I imagined that he had discarded the Armani suit and changed into a thick plaid shirt, like the one he was wearing when I had seen him earlier in the day.

Calum's voice interrupted my thoughts, "Isabelle, you look like you're a million miles away."

"Oh, no, I was just looking at the stars and thinking about Joe. Did you stay in touch with him all these years, Gilles?"

"Actually, no. After he was fired, I lost track of him for years. Nobody knew where he'd disappeared to. But, a few years ago, I ran into him completely by accident. He was dressed like the Mad Hatter from *Alice in Wonderland*, riding a purple bicycle and pulling a doghouse on wheels behind him. It was quite a blow to see how far gone he was. It was as though he was in another world. But, as soon as he saw me, he acted like only a few days had gone by, asking about my painting and how business at the store was going. For the first time in months I took great pleasure in telling someone that the store had gone under."

"How did he end up in Halifax?" I looked over at Sonya when I heard her question and noticed that her arm was tucked into Gilles'. I smiled but didn't say anything.

"I started taking Joe out for the occasional breakfast when we were still in Montreal, but, when I decided to move here and told Joe about it, he seemed sort of interested. He'd heard that Halifax had mild winters. So I ended up springing for his train ticket to come with me. But when I arrived at the train station that day, Joe never showed. Then, a couple of months ago, I ran into him in front of the Halifax library, and that's how we ended up running into Isabelle that day at the coffee shop. Turns out, he'd exchanged his ticket so he could go into detox first. I don't think he's touched a drop since."

"That's quite the story. What do you folks think? Isabelle, have you had enough night air for one day?" Calum looked like he was getting cold.

"Just about. We still have to howl at the moon though. You guys ready?" I cupped my hands around my mouth and began howling with gusto. Sonya and Gilles joined me almost immediately. Even Calum couldn't resist the peer pressure and did some howling of his own.

•     •     •

Not much later I was snuggled under the blankets. The amorphous woman was back in my dreams for a visit. This time she spoke to me directly: "Go back to the Garden of the Gods." She spoke in a stern yet ethereal voice. She paused. Then as if she could read my mind, continued, "Open your heart and prepare yourself for forgiveness. Don't worry, I will guide you."

Before I could formulate a question, the vision faded and began floating towards the window and the full moon.

"Wait." It was all I could think of. She turned one last time before disappearing into the night. In that fleeting moment I saw her eyes, and what reflected back at me made me sit bolt upright in bed.

Howling at the moon, 2000

*Chère* Terry,

That little window into your past was delightful. It made me realize that our emails have revealed more about me than you. I'm glad we made that pact about including stories from our past. I'm getting to know you better already. I will try to rent that Cuban movie the first chance I get. In the meantime, I will continue my own little saga:

My parents were married less than a year after they met. My father began proposing a couple of weeks after their first dance. Mam resisted at first because she still had a year of schooling left before she could start teaching in the one-room school that she had lined up. But my father was always a stubborn man (another one of those traits I'm afraid I've inherited). She, of course, made reasonable excuses to delay, but he would shrug them off (noting her coyness) and head to her father's secret moonshine shed. He would always bring along his largest catch of the day and present it to his future father-in-law.

It didn't take long for my grandfather to agree it was destiny. With the same iron fist that had forbidden my mother to learn to play the fiddle, while he encouraged his sons to play, he proclaimed: "You will marry this man before Christmas or you'll have to find another roof over your head."

Yes, sir, my mother was no fool. She may have portrayed herself as innocent, but even my father must have sensed he was marrying an intelligent, practical and hard-working woman. Nothing less would have done, since they both agreed on having eight children.

On the day of their wedding, it rained like verses of poetry falling from heaven. It was a sure sign that their wish for all those children would come true. And it did — although I am technically number nine. Had it not been for the crib death of one child, I would never have been conceived. Destiny? If destiny brought my parents together and allowed me to be conceived, how can I not be humbled under its spell?

— Manouche

PS    Had another dream about the woman at the hooking frame. This time it was much more disturbing because she gave me a message. She said I had to return to the Garden of the Gods with forgiveness in my heart. I'm positive I've never been to this garden — think I may be going nuts!

Paris, November 2

*Chère* Manouche,

Sorry but this is going to be a rather short email. My brother and cousin are still here. It's been a whirlwind tour of Paris and I have to sleep soon — Germany tomorrow. I'll see if I can stay awake long enough to hit the high points. We took a drive out to Giverny for brunch yesterday. Not as impressive as in the spring but still breathtaking. I scanned a photograph of us in Monet's garden. I'm sending it to you as an attachment. I'm the one with the dark hair.

Your dreams are getting more interesting. When I come back, I will surely have more questions for you.

For now, I'm kind of curious. If you did have to murder someone how would you do it? Given your murder mystery weekend I'm sure you'd be very creative. Or, given your past, maybe you'd be straight to the point. Either way, I'd be curious and even a little relieved to know your preferred method, so that I might guard against it on the off chance I garner your disfavour. As for mine: That's simple — an AXE!

Terry

# CHAPTER 11
## Did We Learn Anything from the Daughters of the Revolution?

After a restless night, I had just fallen into a deep sleep when there was a knock on the door. Francesca came in, followed by Sonya. Francesca announced that they were leaving, claiming they had plans in the city. Obviously their little spat wasn't quite resolved, and Francesca had plans for a conversation in the car. Francesca considered driving to be a sacred time for discussions. In the car, nobody could leave until she came to a full stop. Francesca rarely came to a full stop — not even at stop signs.

I was so preoccupied with the dream and the unforeseen contingency of MY OWN EYES peering at me from this apparition. I couldn't have sounded very convincing in my pleas for them to stay longer. If Francesca noticed anything, she didn't let on. Before they left the room, I told Sonya that I was feeling a little hungover and might not be down until lunchtime.

Sonya left agreeing to keep the lions at bay while warning that I might hear hammering on the roof and downstairs. Somebody's cousin's uncle was dropping by to clean the eaves and replace some rotten boards on the deck before winter set in.

The minute they were out the door, I reached for my purse and took out a notebook and pen. On a blank piece of paper, I wrote:

Questions:
1. Who is this spectre and how is she connected to my paintings or my hooked rug? Or to the roles I'm playing in *Smoke Damage*?

2. Why does she have MY EYES? Is she another alter-ego like Neurotica and Erotica, or perhaps a relative????
3. What about Terry? I can't believe I'm starting to have feelings for her? It doesn't make any sense. Can a person actually become bisexual? Should I do anything about it? If so, what should I do?

Once I had them written down, I stared at the questions. But after a few minutes I got no miraculous revelation or intuition. The only conclusion I had reached over the weekend was that I had better keep Erotica far away from Calum. It was increasingly apparent that this attraction was a twisted desire for his brother, one I didn't have the guts to explore.

What would Francesca think if she knew about that or, for that matter, that I was developing feelings for a woman I had met on the internet? This was just the kind of thing Francesca would flip out about. No, I would have to sort this one out for myself.

I decided to push away all thoughts of men and women, real, virtual or visionary, and reached for the pile of books stacked on the nightstand by the bed. That's what I could use, a diversion to give me some distance and a new perspective, a completely fictitious account of somebody else's life and problems. I picked up a detective novel and turned it over, but for some reason was drawn to a paperback called *The Splendour Falls*.

It was the kind of book I usually shunned with contempt. It claimed to be historical fiction. And since history was my speciality, I normally got frustrated with such blatantly romanticized versions of so-called history. I glanced disparagingly at the author's profile cringing with the memory of Craig's earlier accusations of my holier-than-thou attitude. To my surprise, I discovered that this woman was born in the same year I was. Returning suspiciously to the cover, I concluded that it was no doubt another formula romance, but decided to read the first chapter in order to find out how other people my age were spending their time.

A couple of hours later I became distracted by the sound of hammering outside. By then I was skimming more than reading, when I came upon a captivating dialogue. It was so bizarre that I reread it:

He didn't ask me what I did for a living, but then the French didn't ask such things, as a rule. It was considered impolite, a means of pigeonholing people before one really got to know them. Since the Revolution, everyone was *meant* to be equal anyway.

I couldn't believe my eyes. After more than twenty years of having asked my father a question, I finally might have my answer. I remembered the day as clearly as if it had been yesterday.

I am perched on my father's knee. He has just finished rolling a cigarette that he's handed to the man sitting across from him at the kitchen table and then begins rolling a second one for himself. He rolls the cigarette with agility using the thumb and index finger of one hand. I ask the man across the table whether he fishes with Papape and when he replies that he isn't a fisherman, I ask what he does for a living. Papape interrupts me and tells me that it is impolite to ask such questions. This declaration baffles me to no end, since Papape is usually very supportive of my inquisitive nature.

As the men continued their conversation, I puzzle over the many questions I've asked of the litany of guests my father has brought to the house. Even when I pressed for explanations from a magician he brought to entertain me, Dad's reaction was a proud and deep-bellied laugh.

*"Mais Papape, je'n comprends pas. Pourquoi est-ce que c'est impolie de demander au monsieur son métier?"*

*"Un jour, ma p'tite tu iras à l'école et pis t'étudiras la Révolution Française et pis là tu comprendras. Asteur, t'as les oreilles trop fraîches."*

According to my father, my ears were too fresh and one day when I studied the French Revolution I would understand. To this day, as much as I adore my father's memory, I still hate the expression, "fresh ears".

"Hey, there, you sure look like you're having a nice, relaxing morning." I nearly catapulted from the bed. The voice was coming from the bedroom window. "Oh, sorry — I didn't mean to startle you. I'm Joyce's uncle and I'm here to clean the eaves."

I had forgotten how people outside the city spoke to everybody and anybody no matter how awkward the situation.

"Oh, yes, Sonya told me. I was just about to head downstairs to make coffee." I was grateful that my kimono was hanging on the bedpost. I slipped it on as inconspicuously as possible.

The uncle stuck his head all the way in the window and extended his hand towards me.

"The name's Johnny. Sonya told me you were feelin' under the weather." Johnny winked as though we were conspiring about something. He continued, "I made a real big pot of coffee just in case. So help yourself. Might even take a break in a few minutes myself." *Great*, I thought as I shook his hand.

"I'm Isabelle."

"Sonya told me to tell you that they were gone for a gadabout downtown and would probably end up for lunch at Magnolia's in case you change your mind and wanna join 'em."

"Oh, okay. Thanks."

As I headed downstairs I thought again about my father's words. It seemed unrealistic for a man who didn't complete high school until he was enlisted in the army to refer to the French Revolution with any authority. It was quite a leap to think he was speculating upon the beliefs of the French after the Revolution. It wasn't even possible that it was passed down through the generations since our ancestors had left France before the Revolution, hadn't they?

I was suddenly ashamed at how little I knew about my own history, especially the life my ancestors had led in France before they came to Canada. My area of study was very specific; my thesis was about Neo-Imperialism in Latin America and how 20th century novelists of magic realism portrayed the social impact of this clever shift in subjugation. Whether I was immersed in his tale of unrequited love *Love in the Time of Cholera* by Gabriel García Marquez or his masterpiece *One Hundred Years of Solitude*, the same question came back to haunt me. Did we really have to let go of who we were in order to become who we will be? In a strange way this question was as pertinent to my history as it was to Latin America's.

Last night's vision or dream could have been my subconscious affirming a desire to find out more about Acadian history. Maybe I should ask Terry to check out some of this in the French records in Paris. Better yet, I could go to Paris and check it out for myself.

I now realized why my father had been uneasy with my questions about that man's job. He was a bootlegger who also had a rather notorious reputation in Chéticamp for allowing prostitutes to live in his boarding house. This, of course, meant he was judged harshly by many locals (particularly the women) as encouraging sinful behaviour within the community. His boarding house was also the source of much gossip, especially when the married men of the area were seen entering or leaving the premises. The men would insist they had just dropped in for a minute because they'd missed the liquor store and wanted a quick beer. And, to think this usually happened on Sunday!

As I poured a rather weak-looking coffee, I chided myself. My father would never have provided me with all those opportunities had he suspected they would turn me into a snob.

"Excuse me, Miss. I think we might've just blown a fuse out there. Any idea where the fuse box is?"

"Uh, just give me a second, I think I saw it yesterday when I was decorating the house ..."

After a few minutes of searching, finding and fiddling with the fuse box, we concluded that Sonya's wiring was from a previous era. "Well, I guess I'll just have to send Randy down to get some fuses at the store." He headed out only to return a few seconds later.

"So, you're not from these parts, are ya?"

As Johnny poured himself a coffee, I was thinking, *Oh, no. Not this conversation again*, ast out loud I replied, "Nope. I live in Halifax, but I'm originally from Cape Breton."

"A Cape Bretoner, eh? Never woulda thunk it. So, what part a Cape Breton are ya from?"

"Chéticamp." This time I tried to put a little enthusiasm in my voice. After all, this guy seemed very nice and he didn't know that I desperately wanted some peace and quiet. Besides, my father always said that everyone should be listened to. I wished that I could be as nice as my parents were.

"Chéticamp. Well, what do you know — I ain't been to those parts in years. But, I still remember when I was working the roads, I boarded in Chéticamp many's a time. I used to stay with a nice, old guy named Frankie. Ever heard of him?"

My jaw fell as wide as the Grand Canyon. *That was the man I'd just been thinking about.* What were the chances? I felt a shiver run down my spine and had the strangest sensation, as if I could feel my father's presence in the room.

— *That's it, Mother, you've gone too far. I don't need to know the whole story.*
— *Really, now. I question whether this sudden change of heart has anything to do with your bad judgement. Do you think it was a good idea to bring your daughter to a "parlour" that was run by a bootlegger?*
— *This has nothing to do with me any more, said the son.*
— *That's right, said Patronille, but it does have something to do with me. And, I want to see this story unfold. Now, stop interrupting.*
— *You two are ganging up on me, the son mumbled to himself in resignation.*

"Hey, you look like you just saw a ghost. Was old Frank a relative of yours or something?"

"Uh, no, I …"

"Well, I even have a souvenir of my days in Chéticamp. Frankie used to sell anything and everything on the sly as well as booze. He reminded me of those gypsy folk who used to travel in caravans and he was good to boot. I think he could've sold a coffin to a dead man. Anyway, one of those times when I was really drunk, I bought a small hooked rug of a naked woman. I have no idea what made me buy it. Come to think of it, I had to throw it out when the wife and I got married. She didn`t like it much, I guess."

I was in such a state by the words coming out of this man's mouth that I could hardly bring myself to ask him anything. How could he have thrown it out? When I finally came around I asked him instead, "Do you have any idea who this woman was?"

"Who?"

"The woman in the hooked rug?"

"Nah. Haven't the foggiest."

"Any idea who hooked it?"

"Nope. Don't know that either. Dollars to doughnuts, old Frankie's the only one who'd know that and he's pushing up daisies from six feet under."

"Shit." And then realising I had said it out loud, "Sorry, I didn't mean to say that, it's just that being from Chéticamp, I'm very interested in the rug-hooking thing, you know." But even as I spoke, I knew it sounded lame.

"You know, there was an artist or a hooker staying there at the time. Nice-looking blond thing. I think Frankie said something about her being from New York. He might've even said she was somehow connected to the rug, but I can't be sure. Even if he did, I couldn't tell ya if he meant she was the hooker or the hookee." Uncle Johnny laughed at his own joke.

As my thoughts raced all over the place absorbing this, Calum, Sonya, and Gilles walked in. Turns out, the place they'd picked for lunch was closed and they'd decided to head back instead and eat some of the leftovers. Unfortunately for me, their arrival also marked Uncle Johnny's disappearance.

We made lunch and stuck around long enough to do the dishes before I began packing up. I was feeling a bit guilty that by leaving I would be separating Sonya and Gilles, who seemed to be getting closer by the minute. It was then that I noticed the absence of Gilles' bags. I looked at them with a knowing question.

"Oh, yeah," said Sonya, "Gilles decided he would stay on for a bit and we might do some painting or something. We ran into Philippe on our walk and he mentioned he'd be heading to Halifax later, so Gilles can get a drive with him."

Damn. I had missed Philippe. I had been secretly hoping that he might make an appearance. It was too late to suggest that I stay on as well. Suddenly, I had the strongest urge to scream.

"Isabelle, are you sure you're okay? You look kind of pale?" Gilles was very perceptive.

"Oh, yeah, I'm fine. I think I just drank too much red wine last night. Though someday, when I figure out all this madness, I'll definitely let you guys in on it."

"Did you have another vision, Isabelle?" Perceptive and straight to the point this Gilles was.

"A vision?" This time it was Sonya's turn to be surprised.

"Actually, I have been having disturbing dreams. Gilles, when you get back in town, will you give me a call? I think I'd really like to have that coffee." For some reason, I thought that Gilles might be able to shed some light or at least add a fresh perspective on all this.

"Sure, I'd love that."

"Sonya, thanks so much for the weekend and for the beautiful painting! The murder mystery was a blast."

"Hey, don't thank me — you're the ones who brought enough food for an army. I dare say I'm gonna have to stay here for an extra couple of weeks just so I can eat it all."

After thank yous and a few parting hugs, Calum and I headed back to Halifax. Erotica stayed in Lunenburg and I found myself with some other alien persona. As much as I tried to be civil, I couldn't muster the energy to respond whenever Calum tried to start a conversation.

After a while he gave up, and I just stared, noticing that my eyes reflected back at me from the window against the sky and thinking of the woman from my dreams. I started wishing that Terry were here in person instead of online. With the possible exception of Gilles, Terry was the only person who never dismissed my strange experiences as too creepy, or worse yet, endearing.

I also pondered my father's allusion to the French Revolution. He would be disappointed with the way things were going on the planet these days. Everyone around, including me, seemed to put so much stock in careers and the acquisition of wealth. Gilles could say all he wanted about Chéticamp, but that didn't erase the beautiful memories of my childhood, teenage boredom aside.

Whereas today, people seemed to consider a trip to a Wal-Mart as a family outing, I had grown up with something far more meaningful. In those days, there were no Wal-Marts or McDonald's polluting the countryside with their endless slogans. Instead we went on Sunday drives, picnics, and camping and fishing.

Even the *Mi-carême* tradition, which was a cross between New Orleans' Mardi Gras and the Newfoundland tradition of mummers, had been sadly transformed. People had become more preoccupied with preserving the shine of their hardwood floors than with customs or rituals, no matter how beautiful they were.

"I remember hearing once that the only two sure things in life were death and taxes. Well, they forgot change. And I don't mean nickels and dimes either. Things never remain the same. I know that we're all supposed to embrace change and all that phoney-baloney they try to sell us all the fucking time. And, I'm the first to agree that some change is good. But all the 'buy, buy, buy and you'll be happier' is a load of crap as far as I'm concerned. There, I've said my piece and now I'll shut up."

If Calum was the least bit surprised by my sudden rant, he hid it well.

The only practical thought I had all the way home was that since I had been away this Sunday, I would call my mother the minute I got home. I wanted to ask her if she knew anything about an artist from New York. This tradition of calling my mother every week was one nobody except God herself could take from me. For some reason even thinking of God as a woman offered me no comfort.

Not five minutes after getting home, I got the first real break in my little rug mystery.

Halifax — November 6, 2000

*Chère* Terry,

Well, the hooked rug thing is starting to unravel, I think. I'm convinced more than ever that I was meant to find it. I ran into a carpenter at Sonya's who had been to Chéticamp years ago and bought a similar hooked rug. He told me that about an artist from New York that may have hooked his rug.

When I got home, I called Mam who told me the woman from New York was Lillian Burke. She was a friend of Alexander Graham Bell, who also lived in Cape Breton. Did you know that? Anyway, she came to Chéticamp in 1927 and is credited with the turnaround of the rug industry because she introduced it to the American market. Since she visited Chéticamp when Mam was a baby, Mam didn't know anything else about her. Looks like I'll have to wait till Xmas before I can verify any details connecting her to my hooked rug.

Mam also said she had finally decided to sell the house because she is getting too old to take care of it. I couldn't tell her how desperate I am for the house to stay in the family, at least until I solve this rug mystery.

This is the house where my parents fell in love for the second time. I should know because I watched it unfold with much marvel. It was also where Mam told us about my Papape's most romantic gesture. You will read about it when I send you the story about Papape's funeral. While my more practical siblings were making the arrangements, I remained completely crippled by my loss. Even with John at my side, I was unable to cope. Years later, that entire week remains a complete blank for me with the exception of one conversation that took place on a hot July afternoon on the veranda. And for that, I have John to thank because he recorded it for me. His short story is one of the treasures for which I am eternally grateful.

*Chaleureusement,*
Manouche

PS     Thanks for the photos, although I really didn't need any clues to pick you out. The freckled guy must be your brother and your cousin has a great smile though he's not as handsome as your brother. Is your brother single, by any chance? And you, Terry, are just as beautiful as I had imagined.

PPS    Found a quote on the weekend: "Being is a mystery, being is concealment, but there is meaning beyond the mystery. The meaning beyond the mystery seeks to come to expression. The destiny of human beings is to articulate what is concealed. The divine seeks to be disclosed in the human." The writer was referring to astronomy, but I see it as a sign ...

Paris, November 8

*Chère* Manouche,

I'm sitting at my favourite café reading your email about that carpenter and the connection to the hooked rug. I can hardly wrap my head around it. Is synchronicity really conceivable? It would, after all, mean you and I were meant to meet in this virtual world.

Oops, people I know showed up at my table, big gab session. Gotta go. Talk to you later.

Terry

## Chapter 12
### An Unholy Can of Worms

Gilles was reading from my bible-black journal.

"Well, what do you think?" I was sitting across from him at the same coffee shop where we'd renewed our friendship only two, short months before.

"I think it's quite beautiful. I assume the woman you refer to is the one you've been having visions of?"

"Yeah, sort of, I guess."

"I take it she's still visiting you?"

"Not exactly like she did at first. See, I wrote this last night after I came home from a rehearsal for the play. But I'd never written any poetry before I began reading the script to this play — barring the stuff they tried to get us to write in high school. Anyway, I have the queerest feeling that she's the one urging me to write. Do you think that's even possible or should I just check myself into an asylum?"

"Well, for starters, I don't think an asylum is what you need. Besides, I think you're letting this get to you too much. I'd just go with it and see where it takes you. It's not as if she were coaxing you to mangle bodies, or even start smashing car windows again. Perhaps this is just a subconscious persona that's emerging to help you deal with whatever it is you're dealing with."

"I suppose that sounds plausible enough. Terry said something similar in her last email. But where did you learn so much about subconscious personas, anyway?"

"Believe me, I've had my share of personas. I even underwent psychotherapy to help me deal with my past. At one point, I named them all according to the characters in *The Wizard of Oz*. There was the Good Witch, the Bad Witch, the Tin Man, well you know the cast. Who's Terry anyway?"

"Oh, Gilles, I'm sorry, here I am rambling about my problems ..."

Suddenly, I felt less embarrassed about talking to Erotica and Neurotica.

"No, don't be sorry. It makes me feel useful that you're confiding in me about all this. Besides, my past has no bearing on — you know, we should probably get going if we want to make it in time for the ceremonies."

"Oh, shit, I wasn't paying attention to the time." As we bundled up to leave, I wondered whether Gilles had purposely changed the subject and whether I should pursue it later. I decided to let it drop for the moment.

"Hey, I have an idea. Why don't we pass by the library and ask your friend Joe if he'd like to come with us?"

"I guess we could do that, but are you sure you want him to come?"

"Sure, why not?"

On our way out, Gilles stopped at the counter to pick up a coffee, likely for Joe, and as we approached the library, Joe saw us and waved.

"Hey, Joe, how's it going? Isabelle and I are just on our way to the park for the Remembrance Day ceremonies. Wanna come?" Gilles handed him the coffee.

"Oh, no, I don't need any ceremonies to help me remember anything. But, thanks for the invite."

"Are you sure? We'd like you to come." I thought he might be being polite for my sake.

"I'm sure. Besides, folks seem to be more generous on Remembrance Day. I'd be crazy to pass it up."

"Well, how about breakfast on Saturday instead?"

"Sure, man, you can even bring Venice along if you want."

During the walk to Point Pleasant Park, Gilles asked me again who Terry was and I ended up telling him all about her. I even admitted to Gilles that I was questioning my sexuality because of my feelings for Terry. When Gilles had asked the most difficult questions and sensed that I was getting a skittish, he decided to switch topics and asked about my mother.

"Oh, she's good, I guess. I told her how we'd run into each other. She wanted me to say hi. She's getting older though. Thank God I have a sister who's a saint. Jeannne's being there gives the rest of us some peace of mind."

"Yeah, I have a feeling Jeanne and Adilia are like two drops of water."

I told Gilles it made me angry when I thought about all the intellectual pontificators who wrote themselves into our history books while omitting women like Jeanne and Adilia and our mothers. They're the ones who really sustain the fabric of Mother Earth, not the intellectuals or the politicians.

"Well, I don't know where that little tirade came from, but you do have a point. Don't forget the bishops and the popes of the world, who write themselves in too, while we the peasants have to suffer the insidious guilt they impose on us."

"I take it you're not going to church nowadays?"

"Are you kidding? I've had enough of that bullshit to last me a lifetime."

"Isn't that a tad harsh? I mean, not that I condone all that the Catholic church has done as an institution, far from it, but what about the local church in Chéticamp? Don't you think it's a beautiful reminder of how a community pulled together for a cause?"

"Yeah, whatever."

"No, seriously, Gilles. No doubt you have your reasons. It just surprises me, that's all, especially coming from a man. When I grew up in Chéticamp, I got the distinct impression I was the only one who had a problem with the power of the church over that place. I especially don't remember any men, including my father, thinking it was a problem, aside from it occasionally cramping their style."

"But it's not a man-woman thing at all, Isabelle. It's exactly like you said before about power. I might be a man, but I wasn't exactly the image of the masculine fisherman who would protect his family the way your father did. Besides, don't forget it wasn't that far back when your grandfather was having bidding wars with one of the locals for the front pew. While your family inherited the respect of the church and the parish, mine got lousy Christmas meals and hand-me-downs from its most charitable members."

"Bidding wars? I never heard about that. Not that I want to downplay your experience in Chéticamp either Gilles, but don't forget that if it hadn't been for my stupid temper, the local priest wouldn't have ended up in a wheelchair for the rest of his life. So, I don't think we were quite the favoured lot either. Besides, I totally agree with you about how patronizing the church was, especially now that I know how much money they're worth."

"Wait a minute, back up there for a second. What's this about the priest being somehow crippled by your temper?"

"You and I both know that if I hadn't thrown that rock at your car, Dad would never have been in the car that day as upset as he was. Dad also started drinking after that accident."

"I suppose you're going to tell me that was your fault as well. Isabelle, this is a side of you that's hard to swallow. If you've been carrying this rock of guilt around your neck since that far back, I'm going to have to beat you till you cut yourself loose. Did anyone ever accuse you of this imaginary sin you committed when you were four years old?"

"No, no. It was never like that, at least not my parents. I mean, at first Dad was furious and sent me to my room. But it wasn't long before he came to find me with a box of cookies, crying himself because he'd lost his temper instead of explaining to me why it was wrong. Still, even you have to admit that I was partly to blame for that accident."

"Oh, really? What if I told you that the priest was the one who drove into the side of the car because he was blind drunk?"

"Well that would be convenient."

"It's not convenient, Isabelle, it's exactly how it happened. I should know, since it was my car your Dad was driving. I can hardly believe no one ever told you. Here I thought Chéticamp was the biggest gossiping hole on the planet."

"You know, Gilles, you might have gotten some pleasure from the problems the church was having while I was there this summer. Seems like since we left, some local women have started taking ownership of the church and are making waves about how it's being run. I think there was quite a scandal going on, but I never really got the scoop on it."

"I know you're trying to change the subject, but if you really want me to let this go, you better tell me that you're going to let it go too."

"I will. I promise. This is just a lot to absorb in one shot and, besides, I want to get back to what I was trying to get at earlier. I got the definite feeling you were leaving out some other reason for this contempt of the church and of Chéticamp. Is this, in any way, connected to the therapy you mentioned before?"

"Look Isabelle, it was never a big secret in Chéticamp that I was raped when I was in high school. Not that it was one of those priest cases, but the local priest was one of the halfwits who advised me it was better not to talk about it and to forget it ever happened."

"Oh, Gilles, I'm so sorry, I didn't know. How horrible!" No wonder he was still angry. Gilles was painting the same picture of the Catholic church as I had bitterly painted of Chéticamp in my youth. It wasn't really fair to paint such a picture of an institution because of one human. Of course, this was not the time to point that out. I had come to learn that good and evil weren't labels affixed to any one person or institution. They lived in all of us.

"Don't be sorry. If it weren't for that incident, I wouldn't be the person I am now. I'm more compassionate and I even owe some of the strength in my paintings to that arsehole."

"Oh, God, Gilles, I won't go into my own experience back home, but I will tell you this. I used to rationalize my bitterness too, but a good friend said to me once that nobody deserves to go through something like that in order to become a better person. Gilles, you never deserved to be raped. Don't ever forget that."

I understood the look in his eyes when he heard those words. I had felt the same way when I had heard them spoken out loud. They are the words that every victim longs to hear.

Since the Remembrance Day ceremonies were starting, we huddled together in silence. When the inevitable tears began to trickle down his cheeks, I reached out my hand and held onto his for dear life. It was all I could do. It was all anyone could do.

*For the first time since she began showing her son the story, Bella was infected with Isabelle's human compassion.*

*— Somebody hurt my little girl, didn't they?*

*— I'm sorry, my son, I truly had forgotten that you didn't know. Bella knew that her son would be quiet for a long time. She would remain quiet as well but try to restore his faith in the story.*

Remembrance Day, 2000

*Chère* Terry,

It seems both fitting and ironic that on Remembrance Day I am going to skip the rest of my parents' life together and sum it up with a final excerpt from John's story. It's the part where Mam began to suspect that Papape was building his own coffin.

She considered him now in the light. Even in his illness he'd retained some measure of youth. Indeed, his face was filled with contradictions. Although his skin was grey and wrinkled, his hair remained dark, had only whitened at the temples. And what a boyish expression he contemplated the ice cream with!

He called her back abruptly from these thoughts with an eruptive coughing fit.

"What are you working on now?" she asked as he dropped a Kleenex into the waste basket behind him. "There's nothing more to do."

"That's what I thought too, until last night. I suddenly realised I'd forgotten the most important thing."

"What's that?"

"You're going to have to wait and see."

"It can't be that important." She tried to lead him into giving his secret away. He simply shrugged and replied, "It's important to me."

Throughout lunch they listened to the radio until the obituary report came on. It was something of a ritual. Likely, quite a few of their friends were doing the same. Seeing who could stay alive the longest was the last challenge he could muster. On this day, as always, there was no clear winner.

When he returned downstairs to his work she was still perplexed. What was he working on in the basement? Why was he being so secretive? She scooped his untouched lunch into the garbage can. He was hammering nails now. Why?

He *had* finished with the house. It was in top shape. There was nothing left to build except …

A horrible thought struck her. "Dear Lord, please don't let this be a coffin!"

Thump. Thump. Thump. The hammer connected with a nail.

•        •        •

The storm began with a bellow of thunder. Raindrops pelted the roof. She was gathering clothes from the bedroom closet. She was sorting out a wash. More than forty shirts were hung in a neat row. They were nearly the same, yet each one was subtly different. Some were a different cut, a few inches longer, or shorter, with two breast pockets or with none. Shirts of the exact same make and size differed in colour, sometimes only in shade. These were his Sunday shirts. He may have always appeared to wear the same shirt to Church each week though, in fact, he rarely did.

He truly believed. And yet here were forty shirts. Why did he need so many? Surely God would have settled for two or three.

She wanted to cry as she looked the shirts over. He would not live to wear them all again. Next time he went to church, he should choose the best one. Next time he went to church, maybe she'd have to choose it for him.

"I'm finished," he said, materialising from the mist of her thoughts. He stood in the doorway, a strange, dignified expression on his face.

"May I see it?" she asked.

"No. Not yet."

"When?"

"When the storm ends," he replied.

•　　•　　•

When the rain stopped, he emerged from the basement clutching a miniature house. Seeing it, her first thoughts were "He must be mad." It hadn't been enough for him to make repairs on the house. He'd gone and built another one from scratch.

The storm had ended without rainbow. The clouds refused to yield. He walked through the wet grass to the tree in front of the veranda, began wrapping wire with a pair of pliers around one of its boughs.

After the job was finished, he sat down in a lawn chair to admire his work.

She opened the kitchen door. "Are you waiting for a bird?"

He turned to her and smiled. "I have to be sure this thing works. It's to keep you from getting lonely when I'm gone."

She stepped onto the veranda. "I love you," she said.

He was waiting for the first bird. He was looking for proof that she would never be alone.

"Did you hear me?" she asked.

"Yes."

•　　•　　•

Another grey afternoon, less than a week later, all the children returned home again for the first time in years. In the tree by the veranda birds sang to the reunited family.

How I wish I had written that story. Is it any wonder I am destined for disappointment where true love is concerned? They say every woman looks for her father in a mate. I think my father was the most romantic of them all — rather than starting a relationship with his best foot forward, he saved his most romantic gesture for his last.

— Manouche

Paris, November 12

*Chère* Manouche,

I really (!!!!!!!!) loved that story about your parents. I may have even cried and I'm not usually the sentimental type. The more I get to know about you the more I feel undeserving of your friendship …

Arrived from Switzerland not too long ago. We're back on the road day after tomorrow, this time to my friend, Dédier's place in Brittany. He uses it mostly during the summer months. Did I mention he has a vineyard there? Then, I should be back for awhile since my relatives are flying back to Canada early enough to miss the Christmas madness at the airports here.

I've already unpacked and just put on a load of laundry. I've noticed a fly buzzing about. Did I tell you I had a wasp nest not too long ago? It was interesting to watch. Like the Discovery Channel on my balcony. Don't think I'll ever come up with a story now. Everything I think of pales in comparison to your parents' love story.

Isabelle, let me be frank. I was thinking that we should just end our little challenge. You seem to have such great friends in Canada and I'm just a coward who's better off with books than people.

Terry

# Chapter 13
## Remembrance

On the way home from the park, a fine mist of snowflakes began to dance around our heads and against the Halifax skyline. Gilles and I watched the clouds parting.

"Oh, Gilles, isn't it beautiful? You know the last time I remember having our first snow on Remembrance Day was in 1986."

"You certainly have a good memory." Gilles shot me an incredulous look.

"I usually can't remember what I had for breakfast, but in this case it's good only because of a very romantic gesture my ex-boyfriend made on that night. He'd left my apartment about an hour before the snowflakes began to fall. I was just about to go to bed when he arrived at my door, panting and smiling at the same time. He'd run all the way from the North End just so we could go outside and experience the first snowflakes together."

"Sounds like true love to me. Whatever happened to this guy?"

"I don't know. I guess we both wanted perfection. We were not equipped to handle one another's flaws."

"A tragic discovery."

"Well, I could have said that he was unfaithful and I couldn't forgive him. But I did eventually forgive him. By then, though, I'd matured enough to see that he'd be doomed having to live with my forgiveness. Because I loved him I sabotaged any chance we ever had of getting back together. There's a great line in Margaret Atwood's *The Blind Assassin* about a couple who did just that. For the rest of their lives they shared, "Breakfast in a haze of forgiveness: coffee with forgiveness, porridge with forgiveness, forgiveness on buttered toast."

"You almost sound like you're still in love with him. Could these fantasies of Terry be a way of escaping your real feelings?"

"Great, now you're starting to sound like Francesca."

"Maybe Francesca's right?"

"Wait, there's a funny part to that whole first snow story. We went out to walk in the snow and John, that's the ex, decided we should stop at a corner store to buy some candy for the big event and he bought these godawful things. I could hardly believe they were called candy. John loved them, so I must have eaten half a bag of them — that's how smitten I was. As for me, I'd bought those Pop Rocks — you know that candy that sounds like you're frying it on your tongue. During those first snowflakes, we both put some Pop Rocks on our tongues. It was like fireworks when we kissed. So much for true love and fireworks. At least I'm over that phase of my life."

"Eh, maybe that's what your vision is trying to lead you to, true love?"

"Yeah, right. Well I don't think I'll hold my breath on that one."

"Look, if an old geezer like me can fall in love, why can't you?"

I paused to digest what Gilles had just said. "Hey, wait a minute did you just say what I think you said?"

"Yep. I was thinking about what you said — about the rape and everything. I think it's about time I took a chance on a woman like Sonya. Besides, remember our murder mystery weekend? Well, I told Adilia the night I came back that I had met the woman I was going to marry. Why bother wasting time?"

"Gilles, you are saying what I think you're saying?" Tears were stinging my eyes as I thought about the words he'd used. They were the exact same words Papape had used when he'd met Mam.

"Yep. I'm gonna ask Sonya to marry me this Christmas."

"Oh, Gilles, that's so wonderful. But, what if she wants a church wedding?"

"I don't care about the church that much. Besides, I think I'd marry her in Chéticamp if that's what she wanted. But, don't you even think of breathing a word of this to anyone, especially not Sonya or Francesca."

He looked so happy. For a moment, I wished I could be that happy someday. In my deepest of minds, though, I knew that, for me, true love would remain an elusive memory rather than any future possibility.

"Eh, did you hear me?"

"Yeah, yeah. I won't breathe a word to anyone."

"Well, here we are."

"Oh, that reminds me, Gilles, I was going to tell you about this program I saw the other night on TV. It was part of a Canadian history series and the night I tuned in they were talking about the Acadians. Among other things, they mentioned the diaries of John Thomas, you know the ones that Philippe said he was reading through. They also said the word Acadie comes from some Greek mythology and means Garden of the Gods. Did you ever hear that expression before?"

"No, but then again I might have remembered something closer to the truth, like Infernal Wasteland."

"Gilles, we're definitely gonna have to work on this cynicism of yours. Besides, you know that to forgive someone, or in your case a whole group of someones, is the key to allowing yourself to move on."

"And who are you trying to convince of this, me or you? Aren't you the one who was just talking about the doom of living with forgiveness."

"My point exactly. See, by forgiving them, it becomes their problem, not yours."

"Well, you seem to have it all figured out, though I'm not sure it's that simple."

Of course, Gilles was right. It wasn't that simple.

"Getting back to the Garden of the Gods thing. Remember how I told you that the woman in the dream had spoken to me. Well, that's where she told me to go, back to the Garden of the Gods. Do you think she might have been telling me to move back to Chéticamp?"

"Not unless she's an evil spirit. And I don't think you're having evil visitations. I'll bet you heard that expression before and it's your guilty conscience at work."

"I don't get it. What's my guilty conscience got to do with anything?"

"You're worried about your mother. You might even be thinking you should go home and take care of her."

"You're wrong. I don't allow Catholic guilt to influence my actions." Unfortunately, my lightning speed retort was delivered with a tad too much emphasis.

"Methinks, the lady doth protest too …"

"Yeah, yeah, whatever. Hey, I should really head up. I have some major rehearsing to do for the play — it's next weekend, you know."

"Oh, I almost forgot to give you something." He fished in his pocket and produced two pieces of paper. "Sonya asked me to give you this number of a woman who restores hooked rugs at the market. Seems she broke a leg and won't be at the market for a few weeks, but Sonya was talking to her on the phone and she said that she'd love to talk with you."

On the other one was Philippe's office phone number. "I think you should call him. He seems like a nice guy. Might do you some good." Gilles didn't miss a beat. "He also told me that he and Maria are on the outs."

"If you think Philippe is such a nice guy, why would you want to sic me on him?"

"Uh, I don't know, I got the distinct impression during the Evening of Murder that there were some sparks in the air between you two."

"Oh, you 'in love' people, I don't know about you. I should really go up though. Thanks for the great walk, Gilles. We'll have to do it again soon."

"Yeah anytime. So, you're gonna call him, right?"

"Yeah, yeah, I'll call him. And, if you need any help picking out some flashy diamond rings, you know who you can count on."

"I'm not so sure I want your views on consumerism while I'm shopping for diamonds."

"Hey, even I can be a traditional good old sport when the occasion demands it of me ... although I do hear Cracker Jack boxes are coming back with those prize rings in them. Then there's mood rings, aren't they the new retro rage these days?"

"Right. I'll show you the ring when I find it. Deal?"

"Deal." I gave him a warm hug before unlocking the door.

"Hey Gilles, thanks again for telling me about Père Chiasson's accident. I can't tell you how much it means to me."

"Anytime." Gilles stood there for a moment shaking his head and looking at me with that silly grin of his before he turned and disappeared around the corner. At that instant, a single snowflake determined to defy gravity began dancing upwards toward heaven.

November 12, 2000

*Chère* Terry,

Yesterday, I went to a Remembrance Day ceremony at a local park with my old neighbour, Gilles. After our walk, I climbed up the stairs to my flat and found myself humming that old romantic love song made famous by Louis Armstrong and Ella Fitzgerald. It was the song that John and I used to dance to in our apartment when we were so in love. "Heaven, I'm in heaven, and my heart beats so that I can hardly speak …"

I guess I prefer not to bury my past treasure chest too deeply. Occasionally, on days such as these, I like to peer under its lid, even dig out one of its breathtaking jewels and slip it around my neck. Only, today was a first in that as I slipped into my dreamy, romantic self and swayed to the music in my head, John's eyes were not those I imagined looking deeply into my own. "When we're out together dancing cheek to cheek …"

Maybe there is hope after all.

I finally reached the rug lady, and, although she wasn't sure how much help she could be, she did say that she could date a hooked rug within ten years. I'm so excited! Anyway, we agreed to meet the day after my last performance of *Smoke Damage*. I'm feeling very anxious — can't tell which is more nerve-wracking, the play or the dead-ends my hooked rug keeps leading me to.

Now, Terry, are you mad at me, or something? Your last two emails barely said anything, and then you seemed to be suggesting that we stop the challenge, perhaps even writing altogether. What's up? Are you tired of my stories? I'm trying not to be too shattered about all this, but I really hope you can be honest with me. You kind of sounded like I do when I'm having a neurotic attack and feeling like the whole world would be better off without me. Please tell me.

Perplexed and sad,
Manouche

Paris, November 14

*Chère* Manouche,

Of course, I'm not mad at you and I could never tire of your stories. Just the opposite. I will write a note later and try to explain my taciturn ways. I hope you'll be patient with me while I try to figure out how to tell you what's going on.

Terry

# Chapter 14
## Smoke Damage

"Have you been following the drama unfolding with those American elections?" Sonya asked as we waited backstage.

"What?" I couldn't believe she wanted to discuss politics at a time like this.

"Look, you can't just stand around here getting more and more nervous. We may as well talk about something."

"Well, does it have to be politics?" Coming from me this was rather ironic since this was usually one of my favourite topics. However, today was different.

"Hey, it's the closest thing to theatre I could come up with. Besides, I think there's a great story in that dead guy who got elected."

"A dead man was elected?" Sue, who was playing another witch, interrupted us. "Has he risen from the dead yet to take office?"

"Oh, yeah," Sonya continued, "and then another guy withdrew from the race and also got elected because his name ended up on the ballot sheet. Isn't that something else?"

"Makes sense, I guess. If you leave politics, the public suddenly wants you because you have more credibility." I said. "It just goes to show how jaded the world's become. I'll bet you anything this will become a new strategy for the politicians who are bright enough to notice."

"Isabelle, aren't you the catty one today? Or is this Tart speaking?"

"Sonya, believe me, Tart and I have more in common than you might think."

While Sonya took her usual pause, Jeff, the director of the play, appeared.

"Okay, folks. It's time to take your places on stage. One last thing before you go. Remember how I told you to pull back and tighten your roles before last night's preview performance. Well, forget what I said. Go out there and let it all out. Ready? Let's show them how it's done. Break a leg, everyone!"

I took my place stage left. As the curtain went up, I took a deep breath. My first thought was that the theatre looked full. Word must have gotten around about the reviews of last night's performance. I willed all such thoughts to vacate my brain. This might be the last opportunity for Tart and Rebecca to live through me. One of the more helpful props turned out to be the chewing gum that I gnashed with more defiance than any rebellious punker. It definitely calmed my nerves. Then I spit out the wad and delivered my first line sarcastically.

The next thing I knew it was over. I had only had one Isabelle thought during the whole performance and that had occurred when I'd noticed that Philippe was sitting next to Gilles. But, by that point, I was too engrossed in my role to allow anything external to derail me. The only personal detail I drew upon was my growing belief in reincarnation, which made me more convincing than I might have been in less timely roles.

When I went to the front of the stage to take a bow, I received enthusiastic applause and some hooting and hollering from the third row, where Francesca, Craig, Sonya, Gilles, Philippe and Calum sat. To my surprise, Tony was sitting beside Calum. Then I saw my old high school friend, Caroline. How utterly bizarre to see people from my past and present together in the same room.

Francesca was the first to arrive backstage. She had a huge bunch of sunflowers, my favourite. Not far behind her were Sonya, Gilles, Craig, Calum, Tony, a woman I didn't recognize, and Philippe. They all said nice things. Even Craig was more gracious than usual.

As for Philippe, he was positively hot in a pair of black pants and black turtleneck. His dark hair and strong European features were offset by eyes the palest shade of blue. I imagined how they could belong to a baby wolf lost in a field of buttercups. Strange that our fifteen-year age difference didn't seem all that apocalyptic now that I was over thirty.

"Hi, Philippe, I'm so glad you could come." My heart was pounding and I couldn't tell whether it was because of the play or the present company. All I knew was that I felt deliriously happy.

"You were really great up there. I never would have guessed you were such a talented actress," said Philippe.

"Why, was my performance at the Evening of Murder that lousy?"

"No, no. If I think back to the sparkle you had as a child, I shouldn't be surprised at all."

"Obviously you haven't known her for long enough," said Craig. Francesca shot him a look, but before she could say anything, he redeemed himself.

"You know I'm just tormenting you, Isabelle. Seriously though, you were great up there and we're all proud of you."

"Well, coming from you, I'll take that as the highest compliment."

"Hey, you, not bad for an old bag." Tony gave me a hug that lasted a second or two longer than it should between friends. "This is Lisa, she's a friend of Calum's. I'll be staying with him during our layover, by the way." So he wouldn't be staying at the apartment after all.

In an instant, all the lessons I had absorbed grudgingly came to play. Try to make your smile reach your eyes when the company arrives. Act sad in front of those people who just lost their grandmother. If you can't think of anything nice to say, don't say anything. Keep your chin up when you feel like staring at the floor. Always be nice even when you feel like spitting in someone's eye.

"Hi, Lisa." I recognized her. "I think we've met before, at the Dalhousie Grad House. You used to bring a box of Mini-Wheats with you, right?"

"That would be me. Yeah, that's right — I remember you from Peter's table. You guys were always debating about philosophy class, weren't you?"

"And that would be us. I'm Isabelle." I extended my hand but couldn't quite muster the kind of warm smile that reaches your eyes.

Just then I was tackled by my fellow actors in a group hug. "So, where are we going to celebrate?"

I was suddenly torn between wanting to join the cast for a celebration and spending time with my friends.

"Sonya, you have to come to." Having Sonya come along made it easier. She would help me plan our early escape. I looked over to Francesca.

"No, no — you go and celebrate with the cast. We're all going to dinner at The Fireside, so just go and have some fun and join us for a drink afterward, you know us, we'll probably be there for hours. Besides, Poppy's staying with Craig's parents tonight, so we can stay out as late as we want."

I was hesitating when Philippe piped in. "Isabelle, if you think you might be joining us later, I won't bother going to the car to get a small gift I brought for you."

"Gifts are good. No, no. I definitely plan on hooking up with these guys in an hour or two. If you don't have to leave right away ..."

I was trying to lead him into saying something about Maria, but Philippe just smiled and added that if I was going to be joining them, then he would definitely stick around.

As the cast members ushered me out, Philippe's words were screaming in my brain. If I was coming, he would definitely stick around. That would show Tony!

Instead of joining Sonya and the rest of the cast immediately, as I had planned, I made a stop at home to try to find my lost composure. The only thing I could think of that might put things into perspective was to write to Terry.

My Night as a Witch, 2000

*Chère* Terry,

Have you ever known someone whose eyes are like tiny mirrors that show you the truth when you look into them? Well, I do. And tonight when I dared to look, I saw what there is to be seen deep down. It was as if the most beautiful rainbow you could ever imagine appeared in the sky and being on such a high, I never noticed the stairs in front of me. I automatically began walking towards the rainbow and for a moment it felt like I was walking on air until gravity kicked in. That's when I fell down the entire flight of steps.

His eyes didn't show me what I wanted to see. I saw all the pain I've endured. I also saw a soul who knows instinctively about my anxiety and is trying to understand me. It's as though he can see me from the inside.

Finally, I saw the challenge that lies ahead. As much as something pushes me to walk to him and into the hug he wants to share with me, I will look away from his sad eyes. I just can't allow us to fall under that spell.

On the way home today, I could hear an old song from the '80s playing in my head. "Whenever I fall at your feet, you let your tears rain down on me. Whenever I touch your slow-turning pain …" I kept walking and turned my face upwards in supplication, but my prayers were answered with cold November rain, as if to say that punishment was the answer and not forgiveness. Confirming my suspicions, the sky tossed its clouds madly like ominous waves. In their shapes, I saw that great wild horse of my youth, shaking its mane in rebellion. I saw a metal post and gave in to my darkest urge. Lips on metal, a mess — not so strange, it should all end in one cold taste of bloody steel.

Tomorrow, the mirror in my bathroom will also condemn me with its X-ray — mere bones with the flesh torn away. The long-faded impression of kisses like ghosts floating and unable to land. He will never want to kiss these lips now.

Today I let a parallel universe unfold where Neurotica, my subconscious persona undermines reality. Now I must escape this prison and go join the others at an *après-théâtre* gathering.

Terry, I've been avoiding this topic, but I can't sign off without saying something about your last email. I'm worried about you. I think you came perilously close to forfeit. I am not certain a note that simply states "I'll send you a note later", constitutes a note. I think some gibberish is mandatory. What do you think? Maybe I should take you up on that wager and insist on a ticket to Paris so I can make sure you're okay. Please tell me what's going on!

— Manouche

PS    I can assure you Neurotica has never borne an axe, neurotic — yes; violent — no.

Paris, November 25th

*Chère* Manouche,

I don't know what to say. I could feel my heart sink as I read your letter. I wish I could be there for you. I wish I could stop you from ever being hurt like that again. Am I assuming correctly that Tony is the man with mirrors in his gaze?

A ticket to Paris! Are you seriously considering this? Let me convince you. For one, it is the best place to forget about anything. I should know, since I came here from Québec partly because I wanted to get over my last reckless relationship. Paris has every kind of distraction you could possibly imagine, and I could even offer you some translation work. I'm almost done and want someone I trust to translate my latest work so that it can be used in both English and French universities. Secondly, and back to my concern for you, I would like to see for myself that you are okay.

Of course, you are right to scold me about my poor replies. I promise that I will explain it all soon. It's just a matter of time. So, will you come? As for the plane ticket, I would be more than happy to spring for it if we could look upon it as a partial advance for your translating my work, or an apology …

Terry

# Chapter 15
## The Announcement

It didn't take me long to spot the cast in the bar. I could hear their excited voices the moment I walked in.

"Hey, Isabelle, over here!" Sonya called out.

I pasted on my most radiant smile and hurried over to their corner. I wondered, as I did so, how often my mother had pasted one of those smiles to the world. Damn Neurotica, how could she do this to me today of all days?

Not long after joining them, I started to feel my acting abilities wearing thin. I hugged everyone warmly and made the excuse that I really had to go join my friends because some of them had come in from out of town to see me.

"It wasn't exactly a lie." I told Sonya as we rushed out.

As we made our way down Argyle Street and up Blowers, I was talking myself into making an appearance at The Fireside. Regardless of how much I felt like curling up into a ball and forgetting about the entire world, this was one of those days when I had to rise to the occasion.

Grateful for my silent companion, I watched the fog begin to lift above the Halifax skyline. The temperature dropped rapidly. The frosty chill biting the air was gathering the stony structures of Halifax in a relentless embrace. I shivered and hugged the sunflowers to my body, hoping they would keep warm. The earlier musical notes dancing through my head were flying to heaven with the fog. Would the sun ever illuminate me again? Or, was it all just useless anticipation?

Yesterday I had been reading Anaïs Nin's diaries, partly to take my mind off the play and partly because I felt that Tart and Anaïs had something in common. Anaïs wrote that people who kept old rags, old useless objects, who hoarded and accumulated were also hoarders of old ideas, useless information and even old lovers. Anaïs believed that she had an opposite obsession, that of changing skins, of evolving into new cycles and feeling that in order to learn, one must discard.

"Sonya, do you think that to change internally we must discard objects and people from our past?"

Sonya looked at me blankly. I couldn't tell whether she hadn't heard my question or whether she was thinking it over. Slowly.

In my case, it was true that I no longer spent much time with old friends. Still, I wasn't convinced that this was a prerequisite for who I had become, or was becoming.

"More likely it's symptomatic." Sonya finally answered in that creepy way she had of almost finishing my own thought.

Anaïs Nin threw away everything that had no living, dynamic use and kept nothing to remind her of the passage of time.

"Of course it must be symptomatic because if it were true, how could anyone justify keeping a diary?" I said this mostly to myself. Sonya seemed distracted.

This dialogue was going nowhere. The answers I sought were in my heart, a place better fortified than Citadel Hill, which loomed into full view now. Wasn't it ironic that I ended up living two blocks away from the fortress built to outdo the Fortress of Louisbourg. Arghhhhh!!!

The Fireside was dimly lit by fireplaces and candlelight. As soon as we walked in, I shook off my melancholy as though it were snowflakes on my coat and tried out my smile once again. This attempt was more successful, especially when I noticed that Philippe was still there. He stood up when he saw us. *Chivalry might not be dead after all*, I thought.

"Hey, look who's here? You're just in time for the move. Those people are finally vacating our table by the fireplace." Francesca looked like she was having a wonderful time, though one never really knew with her. She was also a gifted actor, with the possible exception of hiding anger. Neither of us was very good at masking our passionate tempers.

"Yeah, they must have smelled you coming," said Francesca. "You guys should see Isabelle in action. When she decides she wants a table, she just gives one of her looks in the direction of the occupied table and the people miraculously get up and leave."

We were waiting for you before we ordered the champagne. I think this is an occasion to celebrate," Calum announced and signalled to the waiter.

"Actually, I have some more news worth celebrating that I haven't even told a soul yet." I paused for a theatrical moment before adding, "I just accepted a job."

"Really, at what school?" Sonya assumed it was a teaching job.

"It's not with a school at all. As of the first week of January, I will be translating a doctoral treatise in French literature." There, I'd said it.

The waiter arrived with a magnum of champagne and a tray of glasses. Calum immediately took over assisting the waiter to distribute the glasses as quickly as possible. "Here's to Isabelle, to her great performance, and to her new job!"

Above the loud clinking of the glasses and the congratulations, Francesca asked, "Is it at Dal?"

"No, it's at the Sorbonne." These five words were followed by dead silence.

"You mean the Paris Sorbonne?" Francesca recovered first to ask.

*"Mais oui."*

I tried to remain nonchalant, but the atmosphere around me was reminiscent of that foreboding heaviness just before a *suète* would begin ravaging my old native landscape. A *suète* was a southeast gale notorious in Chéticamp for its destructive force.

"Whoa, hold on a minute. When did all of this take place and how come I didn't know anything about it?" Francesca seemed more hurt than happy.

"What's the difference?" Sonya asked, sensing tension. "I think it sounds like a fabulous opportunity and even though we'll miss you,

you can be sure you'll be getting lots of visitors. Gilles, have I told you that I have always wanted to go to Paris?"

"No wonder. Just think of all those art galleries. I think we should start planning a trip right away. Isabelle, how long do you plan to be there?"

"We haven't worked out all the details yet, but I imagine it will be for at least a semester." The truth was I had no idea whatsoever.

There were more toasts and smiles and animated conversation. Francesca seemed to get into the spirit after her initial shock had worn off, although she remained less than her usual vibrant self.

At one rare point, I caught myself gazing out the window at the snowflakes that had begun to dance again. I imagined total silence except for the distant sound of a romantic fiddle. The entire group fell silent at that exact moment. The characters at the table reminded me of a still life. I wondered if Sonya and Gilles, being artists, had noticed.

What was going on behind all those eyes? Each expression so unique but all treacherously approaching serenity. There was Craig, who had given up smoking after Poppy was born. Oh, Craig, who considered his cigarette so dashing, a sign of his masculinity. I was no great inspiration, since I still smoked my Indonesian cigarettes as if I were making love to a man. It reminded me of another era, one when smoking would have singled me out as a woman of the world and a philosopher.

Sitting next to Craig was Francesca, who even in silence, vibrated with cacophonous passions. She was peering, as a lighthouse would, directly at me, through the fog of cigarette smoke. She knew something was wrong, but even her beaming eyes could not illuminate the torment behind my stormy ones.

Then there was Calum, who would be leaving in less than a week and who knew he had been shut out. His own two blue moons were proposing a cheerful invitation to which I feigned ignorance.

Gilles was gaping in wonder and curiosity at us, one by one, the least comfortable with this lapse of verbal diarrhoea. I didn't catch Sonya's look — Gilles was blocking her from view — but Philippe was sitting directly across from me.

Philippe, a stranger to me, really. Still, I couldn't shake the impression that he might be one of the few who was truly capable of seeing the real me, maybe because I had once adored him with the innocent heart of a child. How could I ever make my heart sing and dance again, though, when the fog and clouds of lost love were denying its place in the sun?

I broke the silence.

"So, what happened to Tony and Lisa?"

"Oh, Tony was beat 'cause he got in late last night and Lisa offered him a lift back to my place," answered Calum, looking weary himself. The brothers had likely been up most of the night catching up.

Gilles asked me if I thought Lisa was Tony's type and I replied that she was, if intellect mixed with an off-the-wall sense of humour and a little oddity was his type. "Actually that seems to describe you quite well," Calum said.

"Hey, I'm not that odd. Besides, the one and only conversation I remember having with her was about her desire to grow a penis. Is that odd enough for you?"

"And you only talked to her once?" asked Craig.

"Yeah, an unusual first conversation, wouldn't you say?"

"Okay, so now you've got us hooked," Francesca joined in, "and we know you're dying to tell us."

I was grateful for the change in conversation.

"Lisa used to come into the Grad House with a box of Mini-Wheats every morning, so I had noticed her before. But, on this one particular day, she came in seeming even more confused than usual, and looking around for something or someone. So, on impulse I asked her if she'd lost her best friend."

"Sounds like a question Isabelle would ask of a complete stranger," Francesca said, forcing a smile.

"It seemed like a perfectly logical question at the time. She told me she didn't know where she went. Since I had no idea who she was referring to, I told her maybe her friend was invisible. At this point, Lisa asked the bartender, 'Peter, have you seen my invisible friend.' "

"You know, Isabelle," Craig interrupted, "I'm thinking that so far your little tale makes you sound further off your rocker than Lisa. Who asks people whether their friends are invisible?"

"Let her finish. I want to hear about this chick's fascination with penises." Craig's spoken thoughts resulted in a kick from Francesca.

"Anyways, instead of answering her question, my friend Peter asked Lisa what she was doing with his clothes on. I think he just meant that she was dressed like a boy, but I can't be sure. That's when Lisa told Peter that she wanted to be just like him when she grew up. In fact, she added, she couldn't wait to grow a penis."

"Let's have a toast to Lisa. May she find her elusive penis!" Craig was almost shouting. The champagne was kicking in.

Not long after that I yawned on purpose. "Guys, I really have to head out, I'm exhausted." Francesca looked at me suspiciously.

"So, Philippe, if you don't mind …"

I was hoping this would be a good time for Philippe to lend me the journals we had discussed at Sonya's.

"Oh, not at all, I should head out soon anyway." He was already up and buttoning his coat.

I thanked everyone for coming to the play. We all made plans to meet at my place Friday night for dinner before Calum left for Montreal.

Blowing a kiss, I headed up the stairs leading outside. Philippe held the door open for me. As I walked through, I brushed his arm and a shiver ran down my spine.

"I think I know what you have for me in the car."

"Really, now. And what would that be?" As he asked the question, he moved a step closer and placed a gloved hand on my back.

"I thought you might have brought the journals in with you."

"Uh hmm, well, you're not altogether wrong." We were approaching my apartment and there was still no sign of his car.

"So, where are you parked?"

"The car is just up the street, but I have a confession to make."

"Oh-oh. Do I want to hear this? I thought I'd left the confession thing behind me when I left Chéticamp."

"Well, I don't think it's too sinful, but I lied when I said the gift was in the car. See, Francesca came along with me earlier to convince your neighbour to let us in and put it in your apartment."

"What? You're not serious?"

"Uh hmm, you'll understand when you unwrap it. I know, you're really tired and ..."

"No, no, I guess if you've been up there already, you won't be shocked by the mess."

"The place looked fine to me." The night had become downright Arctic. I was trying to steady my hands so I could unlock the door.

As we climbed up the steps to my apartment, I could hear the phone ringing. I knew the answering machine was liable to pick up before I could get it.

"Hi there, *bonjour*. You've reached 429-1755. *Vous avez rejoint le 429-1755*. Neither Tony nor I can pick up right now, but if you will kindly leave a message in English, *ou en français*, we'll get back to you as soon as we can. Cheers!"

"Isabelle, it's me, Francesca. I know you most likely have some company right now, but will you please call me at home later. I'm worried about you. Please, please, please call, okay? And, you were really great in that play. I love you and I'm sorry if I wasn't as excited for you as I should have been. It's just that I was shocked and also I'm going to miss you like hell. So please accept my sincere congratulations now on getting the job. Big kiss. Mwah."

"Why is Francesca worried about you?"

"Oh, she just likes to worry."

"Hey, is it just a coincidence that the last four digits of your number are the same as the date of the Acadian Deportation?"

"Believe it or not, that's the number the phone company gave me. The person who gave it to me was positive I had lost my marbles when I reacted with such excitement about a phone number. But enough of that, where is this suspicious gift you have for me? Wait. Let me pour us a drink first. There isn't much choice, I'm afraid. There's red wine or brandy. Which would you prefer?"

He chose brandy and volunteered to build a fire.

In the kitchen, a large wrapped parcel sat on the countertop. It looked like flowers or a plant of some sort.

"Hey, I think I found my present." I reached up to bring out my two favourite crystal snifters. I poured two generous glasses and returned to the living room, where Philippe was crumpling newspaper and looking at my paintings. If he noticed that the women were faceless, he didn't say anything.

"Nice paintings."

"Thanks, you know Gilles is the one who painted that sunflower up there." I handed him his drink and placed mine on the coffee table.

"Really? For some reason I got the impression that most of his work was abstract. We were talking about his exhibition opening before you got there tonight."

"Oh, it could very well be. This is something he painted as a teenager. Can you believe we were once all neighbours?"

I got up, scurried to the kitchen and brought back the parcel.

"Can I open it?"

"Sure. But wait — let's have a toast first. Here's to the timeless conviction of history that the past illuminates the present."

As our glasses clinked, our eyes met. No, it wasn't my imagination; the attraction was mutual. That thought made me leap to my feet.

"That was an inspired toast."

On the way back from the fireplace, where I'd poked at the fire nervously, I picked up the parcel and glanced questioningly at Philippe.

"Go ahead, open it."

Inside the wrapping was a grey pot with carved women dancing all around it and a beautiful peace lily planted inside.

"Oh, my God, Philippe. It's absolutely breathtaking. I love it. But, you really shouldn't have."

"Well, I'll be honest and confess I didn't buy it with you in mind. But Sonya came over the other day to invite me to the play and when she saw it, she commented on how the women on the pot reminded her of a cross between a pagan dancing ritual and the statue of Évangéline. So, I thought it would be an appropriate gift, given both your role in the play and your heritage."

"It's true. They do sort of look like Évangéline. And the peace lily complements it perfectly. Here's a toast to making peace with history."

"Hear, hear." The toast was followed by a rather long, uncomfortable silence and then a crackling in the fireplace startled us and we both started to speak at once.

"Isabelle …"

"Philippe …"

"Sorry, you go ahead."

"No, no, ladies first."

"Oh right. The pot, and making peace with history. Here's the short version. I've been obsessed with solving this mystery about a hooked rug I found in my family's house and I guess I'm worried about what I might uncover. But, I guess what I was just talking myself into was that I am not bound to repeat the mistakes of my ancestors."

"If my opinion counts for anything, I don't think you seem the type to mindlessly follow anyone's mistakes, ancestor or otherwise."

This opinion was followed by a look, and then a kiss. The next thing I knew, I was leading him to my bedroom.

Halifax, November 27<sup>th</sup>

*Chère* Terry,

News flash! Decided to take you up on the offer, if it's still open. I'm still planning to leave next week to spend Xmas with the family. Thought I might fly into Paris in time for New Year's Eve, unless that's inconvenient for you. I'm so excited, I even made a tentative booking!

I've concluded that there's some stuff I need to figure out that can only resolve itself by my going there in person. I won't have access to email at Mam's, but you can always try snail-mail! Now, since I didn't forfeit my end of the deal, I'll include one last story for the record.

Prelude: Robertson Davies has always been a favourite author of mine. During my undergrad, I read *Rebel Angels* and, at the time, identified with the female protagonist, Maria. The novel also had many parallels with stories of Rabelais, which really struck a chord with me because Papa used to tell me about these Gargantuan giants when I was young. Well, that novel has always been a sentimental favourite.

So, here's the story: I was on a holiday in Europe, and I'd brought along my last Davies novel to read. I was relishing the idea of how I might find a perfect spot and delight in it without any of the daily working-life distractions. I found it. The café was called Rabelais, reminiscent of the first novel I had read and providing just the symbolic book-end for me to read the last novel.

Rabelais was one in a group of cafés in a town square and there was all kinds of music around, jazz, gypsy guitarists and a group of local folklorists who had had way too much to drink and provided a little cacophony. Since I grew up in a house where music played all the time, I can tune in and out at will. Thus, I read the last Davies novel there was for me to read, or so I thought.

When I finished reading, I set the book down on the café table. I was partly satisfied at having just read a good book but also sad knowing there weren't any books of his to read and that he was quite old now and might die soon, and so forth. Anyway, there, on the table, was a gazette (the kind you find on café tables).

So tell me: What are the chances of a paper turning up on a café table in Luxembourg with ten or so articles, one of them being a review of the newest book by Robertson Davies?

Becs,
Manouche

Paris, November 29

*Chère* Manouche,

I can hardly believe what I just read, I'm afraid I'll have to reread your story about Davies because all I could think of is that you are coming to Paris!!!!!!!!!!! There is so much I have to tell you before you come, but I can do that later. For now, I think I'm going to go dancing so I can celebrate.

Does this mean you'll also translate my work? You know, of course, that you can stay with me in my tiny flat (I have one of those sofas that converts into a bed), but in case you'd rather, I can reserve you a room at the university.

New Year's Eve is a fabulous idea. I could take you to that gypsy club not far from my place or if you would rather we could walk along the Seine and drink some champagne to bring in the New Year? Besides, I'm sure you'll be tired and jet-lagged. What time are you flying in? I'll reread the note, since you may have already told me.

I promise to write as soon as I've come to grips with myself.

Love,
Terry

PS    I'm also trying to imagine what you're like in person. Are you like your mother or father or neither? I feel as though I've come to know them because of the stories. Perhaps even better than you, the storyteller. I'm not really looking for any answers, Isabelle, I'm just rambling today.

# Chapter 16
## Cooking Up a Storm

I was slamming cupboard doors and chopping peppers with a vengeance. For starters, Tony's newspaper was sprawled all over the kitchen table. It was opened at the classified section where he had circled the apartments he was interested in. He was definitely moving out. In the meantime, it turned out that he and Calum might have killed each other if they had cohabited for another week. So he was back in my flat.

To make matters worse, he had left his work boots under the table. Let's see, what else? Well, instead of being excited at the prospect of cooking a nice dinner together, he had arrived hungover and determined to make as much mess as possible while cooking oatmeal. Now the pot I needed to cook the pasta with was caked with dry oatmeal. Men!

After twenty minutes or so of my raging, Tony poked his head around the corner. "What the hell is your problem?"

"You have to ask?" I hissed back. "How the hell I am supposed to cook with your crap all over the goddamn place? And where did you grow up, in a barn? The least you could do is close a goddamn cupboard door when you open it ..."

"You won't have to put up with my crap for much longer. And besides, why should I bother closing doors and depriving you of the pleasure of slamming them with all that pent-up sexual frustration? The way I figure it, I'm doing you a favour."

I glared at him. Little did he know, I had released all my pent-up sexual frustration the night before and wasn't all that happy with my decision. Tony gathered up his paper and walked out of the kitchen, leaving me to my misery.

I drained the pasta and prepared one single plate. It would be delicious: fresh pasta, tomatoes from my tiny garden, portobello mushrooms and fresh basil. Before sitting down to eat, I poured myself an extra large glass of red wine. I used a glass I normally reserved for Sangria, but why stand on formality — I was dining alone.

It hadn't been that bad. We'd had safe sex. Philippe was very discreet and we both agreed, as mature adults, that it had been an isolated incident. After all, I was leaving for Paris right after the Christmas holidays. Oddly enough, Philippe seemed committed to giving his relationship with Maria another go. Still, none of the rationalizing I went through made me feel any better about my main motivation for sleeping with him. It wasn't as if I'd never felt attracted to anyone before. No, this was about my inexplicable attraction to Terry or to Tony. That realization lay at the root of my mood.

As I yanked a chair back, one of Tony's *bregannes* got tangled with the leg. I picked up both boots, marched to the dining room and flung them into the hallway, where they crashed against the wall.

"You know, you're always a bitch after your plays end their run."

"Yeah, well you're always a bastard, play or not." I muttered this last retort under my breath rather than share it with him. I paused at the stereo and put on a favourite Zachary Richard CD, *Coeur Fidèle*. Maybe some good music would turn my mood around.

Oh, but this was a mood. Mine were like those tempestuous *suètes*. Most of the time a storm carried away leaves without destroying the trees. Only occasionally did a storm get out of control. When it was *débauche*, the fishermen weren't supposed to go out to sea. On the rare occasions they dared to tempt fate, their wives would race around the house splashing holy water on the windowpanes. When my mood was *débauche* I was better off staying at home too. It was Tony's bad luck to be there also, without holy water.

At the kitchen table I ate in silence. How different this was from Mamame's dinner table! My favourite room in the family house had always been the kitchen. It was a huge country kitchen with nine doors leading to almost all other rooms in the house. And almost always it was teeming with family and friends cooking, debating, singing and laughing together. Of course, there were also the nights when we were crying together, but these were people who loved and lost with the same passion.

Yet here I was, eating alone. I put my fork down, lit a cigarette and looked around. The kitchen was exactly how I'd imagined it could look when I had moved in years before, planning my life as a bohemian. The walls, a golden sunflower yellow, glowed magnificently above the white wainscoting. The room's one large painting was of three naked women dancing around a table.

Unlike the other rooms displaying dozens of paintings, the kitchen had only two other small prints, one of a flower-filled table with the caption "*la vie en rose*" and the other of a woman holding a small dog. The woman wore a lovely yellow hat with flowers around the brim. It had been one of my favourites when I was young and ignorant about the world of art.

All the art history classes I'd taken, both in Halifax and later in Italy, had done little to alter my taste. Another favourite was "The Birthday" by Chagall, which had also captured my imagination as a child. When Calum had pointed out all the faceless women in my paintings, he obviously hadn't taken into account the kitchen. Still, there were too many for it to be a coincidence.

Was it possible that I feared being attracted to women and didn't want to see their eyes for fear of what I might feel? Or, since my favourite childhood paintings did have faces, maybe women only lost their heads when they grew up.

The kitchen was the room with the most photographs: a framed trio of me and Francesca that captured our favourite Halifax hangouts, another trio of photos of me with my parents, and then a few other memorable photographs on the fridge door. None of my sophisticated trappings were permitted in the kitchen. Although I owned a laptop, I had a strict rule that it was never permitted to cross the threshold of this room.

I took a last sip of wine, got up and glanced outside to my fire-escape-flower-oasis. This week I would bring in the last of the potted flowers before winter took hold. I had painted the fire escape the same shade of blue that I'd loved so much on my trip to Greece. Although through the summer I was fooled into believing that I lived in a tropical paradise, tonight the reality of my surroundings seemed too unbearable to consider any longer.

The music paused between songs. I heard the familiar sound of Tony's snoring coming from the living room. Instead of washing the dishes immediately as I would have been expected to do in the family kitchen, I just rinsed them quickly and left them in the sink. Then, leaning on the doorframe, I watched him sleeping. He seemed so peaceful. None of the foul-mouthed language, none of the wise cracks, not even a frown.

Between us was the beautiful mahogany dining room table we'd bought at an auction we'd gone to together. It was the same table where I had found a rainbow of Robertson Davies' novels and three candles, left there on the day that Davies died. Tony had done that for me. I had no doubt that Calum, despite all of his sophistication, would never think of doing anything so thoughtful.

I crossed the dining room and went into the living room to the couch where Tony was sprawled. I sat down on the edge of the couch and leaned my head into his shoulder.

"There's no room," he groaned. But as he said it, he moved over and pulled me down so that I was lying next to him. "I still love you, you cranky old bag." But he hardly finished the last word. It was swallowed up with another deep snort of snoring.

"I love you too, you, you…"

But I couldn't think of anything else to add. Instead, I just lay there and wept quietly. Next week I'd be gone and Tony might never know just how much I did, crusty as he was, love him. On this night, the knowledge that he would undoubtedly hurt me if I changed my mind was no comfort whatsoever. Besides, changing my mind would be irrelevant. I knew Tony well enough to sense that he was already falling for another woman. Lisa, the woman who wanted a penis, was about to get her wish.

Of course, that wasn't enough to make me stop Tony when he started unbuttoning my shirt and groping urgently at my breasts in the middle of the night. He told me they smelled like hyacinths.

*Finally, the son broke his long silence.*
*— Mother, will you cut it out with the hyacinths. Maybe she would have resisted.*

— *Don't tell me you're still sanctimonious. Did you completely miss the sexual revolution of the '60s?*

— *I know you're trying to make light of this, Mother, but my daughter has been hurt enough.*

— *And, what makes you think this man will hurt her?*

— *Isn't it obvious?*

— *You're thinking like a mortal again! What am I to do with you?*

— *Never mind him, Patronille said upon reappearing. When are you going to get to my part in this story?*

— *Apparently, my son has come by his impatience honestly. We're almost there. I hope you two will enjoy this last part of the journey.*

December 4th, 2000

*Chère* Terry,

A few nights ago after a horrible mood swept over me like a tempest, I fell on the couch exhausted and listened to Zachary Richard until his call-to-arms song, "Réveille" came on:

*Réveille, réveille*
*Hommes acadiens,*
*Pour sauver l'héritage.*

When I couldn't stand it any more I changed the CD to some soothing gypsy music. That night though, even the gypsies in my dreams challenged me as to whether there's anything worth saving of my Acadian heritage?

The next day, I awoke with that same sour aftertaste I get in my mouth each time I think of how I was denied my right to self-actualize in my culture. Instead, I've been assimilated, a self-actualized Anglo. The difference between gypsies and me is in their ability to divinely transform what they absorb.

Maybe I'm a gypsy whose interests aren't served by blind obedience to rules and traditions created by the sincere desire of my ancestors to preserve what was useful in their time. A gypsy who left the caravan afraid that repressing my right to think freely might result in conformity. Or, am I mourning the moral values and traditions that might still have the power to comfort me?

So, you're excited about me coming?! I should warn you that I'm freaking out about finally meeting you. Expect me to be either completely quiet or to ramble on about nothing. Or I may simply peer at you like a deer in front of a set of headlights.

By the way, as to my character: Definitely not like my mother. She's kind, genuine, and traditional. I am moody, slightly eccentric, and infinitely more neurotic. Tony told me once that I wasn't the kind of woman that a man would marry. He thinks I'm dark and broody. Oh yeah, and that men want to listen to me, to look into my eyes and search for truth, but that they eventually become more spooked than fascinated and want to run away. That could explain a lot. Then again, others say I'm exuberant and funny.

My flight number is 446 and arrives at 3:15 PM. I'm so excited!

Manouche

# Act Three: The City of Lights

*Props:* A mythical garden, a deck of tarot cards and a twist of fate …

# Chapter 17
## The Rug Lady

On the Saturday following the play, Francesca, Sonya and I were finally driving out to meet with the rug lady. Sonya had gotten wind that she also read tarot cards and it was decided that the three of us would have our cards read at the same time. I was a nervous wreck. I couldn't forget that last tarot reading when the fortune teller at the circus had predicted the death trinity of my father, my brother-in-law and my unborn child.

I fidgeted with the radio stations until Francesca produced a tape for the stereo. Then I began drumming my fingers loudly on the steering wheel.

"Oh, for God's sake, Isabelle," exclaimed Francesca, "will you relax. It's not like anyone's forcing you to jump out of a parachute. Just tell her when we get there that you don't want to hear any negative parts in the reading."

"Oh, like that would help. Imagine if she said nothing."

"Just consult her about the hooked rug and forget about the tarot reading altogether," Francesca suggested.

"Not a chance. My life is about to undergo a drastic change. The least I can do is consult the stars about my options. My mother used to say that I was just like my father. When we would get an idea in our head, it wasn't at our feet."

I was relieved to see the snow begin to fall. Now Neurotica could test the wipers. Slow, medium and fast speed. Intermittent. The windshield washer fluid was working. No need to de-ice.

Francesca was navigating. "Isabelle, I think you have to take the next left. Does that sign say *Lawrencetown?*"

"Yup."

"She said we had to drive about five miles, then take the first driveway to the right just past the red barn."

In this last stretch of the road, the snow got thicker and we grew quiet. I was thinking that going to Paris might be a big mistake. In fact, being out here on this country road made me think that I was tiring quickly of city life. Maybe a hut or chalet by the ocean was more what I needed. I began to paint the idyllic little getaway in my mind.

*Springtime would surprise me bursting first with crocuses and then tulips and hyacinths and later with all kinds of wildflowers in the fields. As the days grow longer and warmer, barefoot, I make my way to the ocean as the surf keeps pounding the landscape around me. I become the gypsy I always dreamed of. Later, summer's longer shadows shrink and with this turn the leaves scatter about, gracing the soft earth they came from. November comes and goes but more slowly than the one I'd almost just missed. And the November rains are as cold and incessant as in the city, but here, in the country, I huddle next to the fire and listen to the rhythmic pitter-patter of John at the typewriter, that same comforting sound that made me fall in love with puppy paws and raindrops.*

The realization that John had crept into my reverie made my thoughts shift abruptly. No, Neurotica. No. Not the countryside. A better option would be a small French village with a flower market. After all, I loved human scale, and it *was* possible to daydream without complete regression into that damned parallel universe of obsessive memory. I've never responded warmly to things of giant scale, gargantuan companies where humans get lost or exploited. Much better to visit intimate villages, collect tiny handmade objects, drive small cars or, better yet, bicycles, and drink fair-trade coffee in cozy cafés.

"Hey Isabelle, there's the red barn." I heard the relief in Francesca's voice.

The bright poppy flame stood out against the fat snowflakes. I began easing my foot off the accelerator and could soon make out a mailbox at the driveway just past it. I shifted down and then sped up.

"Careful, it's probably quite slippery."

"Never would've pegged you as a backseat driver, Sonya." The fat silence it caused was like an unwanted passenger. "Sorry, I become somewhat of ass when I'm out driving country roads."

"Well, you're obviously experienced," Sonya said. We passed the one car that hadn't quite made it to the top of the driveway and then pulled up easily in front of the door.

"Here we are girls, safe and sound."

The front door was painted bright orange and decorated with a pine cone wreath. Before we were even out of the car, the door to the house flew open and there stood a short, plump woman with long hair pulled back in a bun and wearing a curious pink apron with orange elephants on it. Her smile was almost as wide as the elephants on the apron.

"I was starting to think you might've changed your mind when the snow started coming down so hard. Come in, come in."

"Hi there, you must be Florence. I'm Isabelle and these are my friends Francesca and Sonya."

At this point we were all stomping feet and brushing the snow from our coats.

"No, no. No need of formalities here. You can even keep your city shoes on since I haven't started my usual Saturday housecleaning. We had the annual Christmas bake sale this morning and I've been run off my feet since sunrise. I just finished dividing all the stuff up for the freezer and the kettle's on the stove. You all like tea?"

We looked at each other and nodded enthusiastically.

"So you're all looking to get your fortunes told, eh? Have you already decided whether you'd rather hear them together or would you prefer private readings?"

"Together!" I answered emphatically and turned to my friends for reassurance.

"Yeah, I think we all know each other pretty well. You don't mind, Sonya, do you?"

"Well, I hadn't really thought about it, but I guess it sounds all right, as long as I don't have to go first. I think I have to get in the mood for a bit."

"I don't want to go first either." This was one thing I was sure of.

"Oh, you two. I'll go first and I don't care who listens in," Francesca said, always the pragmatic one.

Florence paused by the wood stove and poured water from the kettle into a teapot and placed a tea cozy on top of it. She then left the kitchen, presumably to fetch the cards.

"Francesca, are you sure you don't mind going first?"

"I can't wait to hear what she's going to say. What about you, are you sure you haven't changed your mind?"

"Oh no," I said, "I'll be fine. Just so long as she's not all doom and gloom when she's reading yours."

Florence came in and reassured us. "What's all this about doom and gloom? I see only good things, and besides, if I see any doom and gloom, I just advise you on how to avoid it. So, who's going to go first?"

"Me. I'm Francesca." Francesca flashed one of her full-teethed smiles that I instantly recognized as a sign of nervousness. Ah, she wasn't all bravado like she pretended.

"So Francesca, do you have a particular question for us today?" Florence poured tea for everyone and handed the deck of cards to Francesca, indicating for her to begin shuffling.

Around this time, I returned to my daydream. *Like the hut, the village is also by the ocean but it has lovely cobblestone streets lined with old street lamps. The houses seem more like cottages, each one a different bright colour, and with a verandah facing the street. Along the main street are little European pastry shops and bakeries, small carts selling fresh, organic fruit and vegetables, an open-air flower market and many cafés. At a neighbourhood nightclub a lively fiddler or a romantic jazz musician soothes the autumn chill, and occasionally a passing rock band explodes at night. At night the stars and the moon remain impassive, undisturbed and eternal. They console me in my loneliness of living without Tony, who I know deep down loves me. It was so obvious the other morning when he …*

Good God, did it always have to be reduced to men? Couldn't I just be happy as a single woman? It was the world's fault for inundating women with images of happy couples. The big world was just too horrible to swallow, so I would learn how to reject it instead. Perhaps that sounds like refusal to grow, but that in itself, is a phase of growth. On the other hand, maybe it was more of an abdication, a sort of evasion of life to avoid feeling altogether.

I started wishing that instead of sitting through a tarot reading I could be curled up with a good book next to the woodstove. Something by Thoreau that could inspire me and plant a nostalgic seed for an earthier life without the morass of feelings I was injecting into it. Reading Thoreau would be more cerebral. Then again, maybe what I really needed was something less cerebral.

Perhaps this fortune-teller could assist me in arriving at the roots of my own life tree. What made it grow or die, wither or bloom? It was there in the earth, as with all else, that the answers rested, waiting to be uncovered.

"Well, who's up next?" Judging by the look on Francesca's face, it had been a pretty good reading. This time when Florence got up, she returned with a plate of cookies.

"I'll go," I volunteered and then added quickly, "if that's okay with you, Sonya?"

Before I could change my mind, Florence handed me the cards and commanded that I shuffle. This simple act helped me concentrate on something other than Terry, John, Tony, the hooked rug or all the other meanderings my brain was taking me on in order to avoid thinking about them.

"Isabelle, have you come to us with a particular question?"

"Well, not exactly particular. I guess I'm interested in relationships, career and also where I should live … I think that's about it?" I glanced at Francesca and Sonya, who seemed to think these were good questions, so I kept shuffling and tried to concentrate on those questions as I did.

"There." I handed the deck to Florence and held my breath as she cut the decks, finally setting them all in one pile, taking the top one and placing in the centre. It was The Fool!

"Uh hmm." Florence let her glasses slide down her nose as she peeked at me. "You know, you can start breathing again."

I gave her a half-smile, reached for a cookie and started munching on it.

Without pausing, she flipped the next two cards and said, "Ah, The Two of Pentacles and The Knight of Wands. Looks like we're about to make some big changes here, there lots of movement covering you."

That wasn't so bad, at least not on the surface.

The next card she turned was The Chariot and she placed this one beneath the trinity in the middle of the table. I wondered why a trinity would appear in tarot cards.

"Looks like you had lots of positive and happy influences in your past. That's a good thing. You're coming into this period of change with lots of confidence and your eyes wide open."

I knew immediately when Florence turned over the next card that it was not a good one. The Five of Swords. She placed the next card, The Five of Wands, above the trinity.

"What about that last card? Swords are a bad sign aren't they?"

"The Five of Swords in that position refers to what's behind you. It looks like someone did hurt you. I'd say there was deception involved, but let's see if it factors into the rest of the reading."

The next card, The Nine of Pentacles, brought a smile to Florence's face. Her smile widened when The Star card appeared next. I began to breathe a little more evenly.

And then another damn Sword card, this time The Eight. Shit. Things seemed to be going so well. The last two were The Princess of Cups and The Hierophant.

"Well, well, looks like we're moving somewhere for certain. Far away, too, I take it? And there's also going to be a new job."

When I didn't respond right away, she continued. "And look at that Nine of Pentacles. It's telling us that you're going to have a windfall. Now that could be material wealth but not necessarily. Whatever it is, it's good fortune, but its effects could be short-lived unless you manage it wisely. Now it's also followed by The Star, which indicates a burst of inspiration in your personality. But The Star also refers to nerves, so my best advice is to express your creative urges rather than allow more neurotic feelings to take over. Maybe you should try your hand at painting?"

"What about love? Is there anything about my love life?"

"There sure is. We were just getting to that. The Princess of Cups up there is telling you to accept invitations and to do things that you might not otherwise do. There's a proposition in the air, lots of romantic current and deep emotional attachments possible in your future. I would even say that this is connected to all that change and movement. I'm willing to bet that if you haven't already received this declaration of love, it's imminent."

Good God, could this woman be referring to the invitation from Terry? What else could it mean? Francesca and Sonya were just as intrigued as I was with this little piece of information, since neither of them knew about Terry.

"What about that other Sword card?" I asked.

"Oh yes, that deception. I'm getting some weird vibes around that one. It looks like the deception is in the past, but it's almost as if either you weren't listening or you haven't dealt with it yet. Does that make any sense to you?"

John was the only person I could think of.

"Does it indicate how long ago did this deception took place?"

"I would say not very long, looks like it could be five weeks or five months."

"What? I can't think of anyone who's lied to me recently. Does it say anything about the deceiver?"

"No it doesn't, but I wouldn't worry about it if I were you because it's in the past and you should just deal with it and move on. Regrets are a waste of time anyway. Better to just live in the moment." Easy for her to say. I didn't know who or what I was supposed to deal with.

"The other card you were asking about refers to your support network. It says you're going to have to make some choices that people around you may not approve of. You may be feeling hemmed in a bit, but don't let it hold you back. You may simply have to re-evaluate some relationships in light of this new life you're going to choose."

Francesca interrupted, "Well, that can't be us, we'll support whatever you do, Isabelle."

"Did you tell Isabelle anything about the last card or did I miss that?" Sonya asked. She was paying close attention.

"No, I haven't said anything about it yet and I must say that I'm more than a little confused by that card. Now, I'm not always right, but the woman I see before me seems to have very little in common with The Hierophant. You see, The Hierophant is very balanced and conservative. Sort of the stable but stuffy type, all about rules and traditions, if you know what I mean. Now you, Isabelle, strike me as not in the least conservative. I'd even venture to say that you're more spontaneous than balanced?"

"You're right about that," said Francesca, who was sure she knew me better than anyone.

"I think I understand why that card is in my reading." I said. "It may sound crazy, but it makes sense to me."

"What? You've got to be kidding. How on earth do you, Isabelle Desveaux, relate to this card?" Francesca was clearly annoyed.

"It's connected to the hooked rug I brought to show Florence. The way I see it, the rug is a product of rules and traditions based on the sincere desire of my ancestors to preserve what was useful in their time. Even if I don't follow their rules — the person who hooked this rug didn't follow them either — it doesn't mean that their values haven't comforted us in some ways. It doesn't have to be like day or night. There's dusk also, kind of like the mood of the rug."

"Isn't that a bit much for a tarot card to pick up?" Francesca asked, looking at Florence.

"No, think of it: if you're going to move far away, you'll constantly be evaluating other people's cultures and values. It seems logical that you would be carrying your own background with you as a measuring stick of sorts."

I knew that this tarot reading hadn't changed Francesca's mind one bit. She went along for the fun of it, but she wouldn't take it seriously unless there was a bad omen, and that might lurk in her brain obsessively for a while, but otherwise she was a skeptic. Oh, well, *Vive la différence.*

Florence said that before she did Sonya's reading she wanted to have a look at the hooked rug, so I ran out to the car to get it.

When I unrolled it Florence looked baffled and somewhat dismal, but her initial reaction was soon replaced by a slow whistle.

She raised and lowered her eyebrows repeatedly, reminding me of *The Muppets*.

"Oh my, what a lovely piece of work."

After swooning for another few moments, Florence bolted out of her chair and announced that she needed her instruments.

"It is a really beautiful piece, Isabelle." Sonya echoed Florence's words. "You know, if you aren't planning on bringing it with you to Paris, I'd be honoured to take care of it for you."

I hadn't even thought about whether to bring it or not. I could hardly imagine being separated from it. I told her that if I did decide to leave it behind, she would definitely be my number one choice of babysitter.

Florence came back in the room carrying folders, books, and what looked like a regular toolbox. After poking around and staring for an inordinate amount of time through a magnifying glass, she declared that the rug had definitely been hooked long before the turn of the century.

"Now the bad news is that this means there is no connection whatsoever with Lillian Burke."

We all began to wilt together like three flowers deciding to die at the same time.

"However," sensing our disappointment Florence rushed ahead, "this could also mean that you are holding the oldest hooked rug ever preserved in the history of the Chéticamp rug-hooking industry."

"How old are we talking?" Francesca asked.

"Well, I thought I'd be able to date it accurately, but I've never dealt with a rug as old as this. I would say it's at least two hundred years old judging by the dye that was used."

"You can't be serious?" I exclaimed.

"I'm very serious. Not only that but it seems obvious to me that the person who hooked this rug was more likely an accomplished artist than an experienced rug hooker. This might be hard to tell if you just look at the image, but the real mastery in a hooked rug is found by examining the back of it." As she said this she turned the hooked rug around.

"Now, just so I can demonstrate, let me show you a small prize piece that I acquired by Elizabeth Lefort. She's one of the best-known hookers from Chéticamp. You can find her work in the House of Parliament in Ottawa and at Buckingham Palace." Florence was talking from the other room at this point, but now she returned with a rather smallish piece of hooking that she was removing carefully from its framing.

"This is fascinating, Isabelle. Aren't you excited?" Sonya said, obviously excited herself.

"I just can't imagine how such an old hooked rug could have ended up in the family attic. It doesn't make sense. I mean, if it was in the attic all these years, you would think someone else in my family would have found it when we moved in. Wouldn't anyone be at least a little curious if they found this?"

"Look at this, girls." Florence was comparing the backside of the two rugs. Even to an amateur it was evident that the smaller one by Lefort was far neater and immaculately executed. Not a piece of wool was unattached or hanging loose. The image on the back was almost an identical match to the front.

"Does this mean that the lesser craftsmanship makes it less valuable?" Francesca was always the most practical in such matters.

"Well, there are a couple of possibilities here. One is that the rug was hooked by someone in Chéticamp who hadn't yet mastered the art of hooking. If that's the case, its main value is in its unusual rendering and its age. It would likely be of interest to a local museum that might want to acquire it for a modest sum ..."

Sonya, who was usually so slow at following conversations, interrupted. "But another possibility is that someone famous came to Chéticamp way before Lillian Burke discovered rug-hooking. Wouldn't it be amazing if some really famous painter had come to Chéticamp and decided to try their hand at rug-hooking?"

"I'll say, though that's unlikely. However, if there were some way of proving that this piece was hooked by someone of historical significance, it could mean that your hooked nude would have an even larger audience. Think of it as finding the only surviving Picasso but in hooked-rug circles. There are dealers out there who would remortgage large portions of their estates to acquire such a rare find."

"How does one go about proving or disproving its authorship?" asked Francesca, now almost as excited as Sonya and I.

"Start where you found it. There might be some clues in that attic that could really help us establish some leads."

"I want to go with you, Isabelle. I think she's right, maybe we can find something in that attic. Sonya, I think you should come too. We finish school on Friday and we could be on the road by Saturday morning. That's a week from today. What do you think?"

"Well, I don't know," said Sonya. "Isabelle, what about you, what do you think? Do you even want us to come along?"

I didn't know what to think at this point. I had the weird feeling again that this was connected to the woman in my dream. I wished I knew who she was.

I decided to tell Florence about my dream. Then I made a suggestion.

"Sonya, why don't we go back to the table and let Florence do your tarot cards while I absorb all this."

Florence told Sonya that there was marriage in the air and soon. I had to refrain from reacting. Rather than tempt fate by making eye contact with anyone, I pretended to be lost in thought about my hooked rug. It was true to a point. What was bugging me more was my own reading and that The Fool had appeared first. The tarot deck, like all decks of cards, contained a joker-like wild card. I was a bit of a control freak and this card was a reminder of how little control I really had.

By the time we left Florence's place, darkness was beginning to set in. It was the time of day that we call *entre chien et loup*. I wondered about its possible origins. I figured that the dog represented domesticity and therefore safety whereas the wolf was a wilder and unpredictable animal perhaps more akin to the fears of darkness. As we drove towards the city, the small yellow lights I could see peeking above the hills in the distance looked like the piercing eyes of a pack of wolves waiting for us.

*Chère* Manouche,

*Joyeux Noel!* Merry Xmas!

I know the wishes are early, but if all goes according to plan you should be leaving for Chéticamp in the morning. Just a short note this time because the family is all here. Turns out my brother's story was all a ruse so our parents could surprise me by landing here for the holidays. It has been wonderful so far, but that could all change in a split second.

I can't wait for you to arrive for New Year's. Though now that we've shared so many of our tales, what will we have to talk about? I did find something in Paris that I can't wait to show you, but it's a surprise!!!!!!

Deer-like staring activity sounds great to me! Would it be okay to bring sandwiches? It is still okay to eat while we stare, isn't it? Or do we have to be frozen in place like deer? You are very funny.

So Sunday. Give me a call the morning of your flight to confirm the time if you can. Not to worry though, the rest of the family will be on their way by the time of your arrival and I'll even leave my university friends out of it for the time being. You seem so nice; I'll spare you the rigours.

I hope I can get off in time to pick you up, because I'm meeting my doctoral supervisor to give me the final word on …

# Chapter 18
## Seasons of Love

On the Saturday morning following the tarot card readings, I awoke desperately clinging to the image of someone in my dream. An elusive being that I couldn't quite visualize yet who seemed so real. It felt like a deep-rooted yearning for a spirit that was connected to my soul. An achingly sublime music was playing in the background.

I couldn't get that tarot reading out of my mind either. The possibility that fate might have a man waiting for me in Paris was irresistible. If the romance waiting for me had been with a woman, Florence would have said something wouldn't she? Unless of course that was what she was alluding to when she talked about me making changes that some friends would not support.

French or not, there were homophobes in every crowd, just as they could be found in every city, town and village. I thanked my lucky stars that it wasn't exclusive to Chéticamp. Wouldn't that be embarrassing to admit? "Hello, my name is Isabelle and I come from the only village on earth where some folks are more afraid of homosexuals than they are of aliens or ghosts."

The sound of the street below was louder than usual and all kinds of bells were ringing. I opened the window all the way and stuck my head out. Spring Garden Road was brimming with Christmas cheer. At least two dozen Santas were parading with reindeer and bags full of treats for the youngsters. Smiling people stood clustered listening to choirs singing Christmas songs. The day was explosive with sunshine and generosity of spirit. World peace seemed possible on a day like this.

I leaned out a bit further and looked to the board above the sports shop. The temperature read 14° Celsius. Not bad for December. I decided to dress light but wear my winter coat in preparation for Cape Breton's icy winds.

In the Mills Brothers window directly across from mine, the annual "Snow White and the Seven Dwarves" display was already attracting a small group of admirers. Even my Disney boycott couldn't deflate me on this glorious day. It was the one time of year that while living in a commercial district, I suspended my cynicism about living in a capitalist world. Ironically, this was also the time of year when sales were at their highest.

The time on the board read 10:15 AM.

Holy shit! I slept in. The going-away dinner for Calum had ended up lasting until nearly sunrise. Francesca and Sonya would be here in less than an hour and I hadn't finished packing yet. The first thing on the agenda was to see if I could recover Terry's email after last night's brief power outage interrupted its transmission.

When I tried to log on, the system wouldn't let me in. My account had been disconnected on the exact date I'd requested. Damn efficiency! It was a good thing I had Terry's number. At least I could call her from Cape Breton. For now, I had no time to waste.

At 11:05 on the nose, when Francesca's car pulled up, I was already outside the door relishing my last cigarette before the smoke-free drive to Chéticamp. Francesca leaped out to greet me with a hug.

"Oh, this is so exciting. We're off on a Cape Breton treasure hunt."

I reached inside the door to grab my two suitcases and Francesca took them from my. That left only the gift bags piled with Christmas presents I was bringing home to the family. So much for my frugal intentions before the trip to Paris, not to mention my anti-consumerism. But I'm an expert in justifying my decisions. There is, after all, only one life to live and one family to share it with, right? Of course not. I've always believed deep down that the world is one big family and that if people believed this there would be less poverty and fewer starving people. On this day I was in a most forgiving mood, even towards myself.

We made one stop before leaving the city. At the candy store I stocked up on Pop Rocks just in case the tarot cards were right and I needed to start some fireworks in Paris!

The drive to Chéticamp took about five hours. On the way, we took turns sharing our Christmas memories. Although I had told Terry many stories about my parents and childhood, my closest friends knew little about them and I knew next to nothing about theirs.

Francesca had never once mentioned that back in Sweden she had to wear a wreath with lit candles on her head because she was the eldest daughter. So adorned, she had to serve buns and coffee to the rest of her family. Now, this would have been a sight to see!

One thing we all agreed on was the importance of food during the holiday season. It brought to mind the annual Christmas Eve supper I used to have at a friend's house. My friend's mother, Catherine was one of the best *rappie* pie chefs in Chéticamp.

And then, as if that wasn't enough, Midnight Mass was always followed *le reveillon* at the Desveaux household. While filling up on meat pies and lobster sandwiches the family would gather to unwrap the gifts. When my father was still living, that had been *the* climactic moment. Preceded by weeks of ransacking closets, looking for parcels, finding some, jiggling them mischievously, tearing little bits of wrapping paper just to see if he could get a clue and then doing a poor job of taping it back on. He was, like me, an eternal child on such occasions, bubbling over with pure, unadulterated *joie de vivre*.

I held a trio of Christmas moments (there was that darn trinity again) particularly dear to my heart. The first was when the church choir got to the part of "Holy Night" where they sang *"Tombe à genoux"*. Those words never failed to make my knees weak with gratitude at being alive.

The second moment came when I opened a small package from my father. Every year I knew what it would hold. Each year, a new exquisite porcelain bird was added to the tree, the newcomer eclipsing all others in beauty until another year came along and an even more ravishing bird would arrive. When I said that I hadn't received a bird now for eleven years, Francesca began to cry.

"Oh, Francesca, I'm so sorry. Here I am yammering on about all these happy memories and you're not even going to be with your family this year."

"No, no. It's not that at all. It's just what you were saying about the gifts and all. It's so beautiful, that's all. There's something I know but can't tell you yet."

"Should I be worrying about something? What do you mean there's something you know but can't tell me? And why is that making you cry?"

"No, it's nothing like that. There's nothing to worry about."

"Francesca, Isabelle is right, it's not like you to get all emotional and sentimental about holiday memories. Are you sure you're okay? You're not sick or anything, are you?"

"No, I'm not sick." Francesca was now laughing and crying at the same time. "All right, stop the car."

"What? Are you going to be sick?"

"No, I'm not going to be sick. Now will you stop the damn car, please."

I did as Francesca demanded and pulled over. We were at the last big turn before the intersection at the end of the Shore Road. The steeple of the Chéticamp church stood proudly in the distance across the water.

As soon as the car stopped, Francesca ordered me to pop the trunk. Sonya and I followed her outside and watched as she dug through the suitcases for a small bag, which she handed to me.

"There. I know it's early and you weren't supposed to open it 'til Christmas, but I won't be in Chéticamp on Christmas day."

I removed a small box from the bag and glanced at Sonya and Francesca.

"Go ahead, open it."

I unwrapped the gift box and opened the lid and there it was, a porcelain cardinal, as crimson as the sunset that was beginning to stain the horizon.

And that's when we all started to cry.

Once we were back in the car and relatively composed, Fran began telling Sonya about her hard-won victory at matching my gifts. It was true that I went to ridiculous lengths sometimes to give my friends and family a taste of what I'd inherited from my father's romantic nature. Francesca's family, I discovered, had a tradition of giving a book and a rose to each of the women on World Book Day. It was a custom that her ex-husband picked up when they married.

On the first World Book Day following Francesca's divorce, I showed up on her doorstep at seven in the morning holding a rose in my teeth and a book in my hand. One of the thorns had pricked my lip and with a bloody kiss mixed with the salt of our tears we became blood sisters.

By the time we crossed the bridge in Margaree, the sun had almost finished its descent, sinking to an ever deeper red as we drove past lakes and ponds. Grand Etang, the largest pond we passed, was also the name of the community where my older sister Jeanne lived.

As we approached Jeanne's house, I started to slow down. Noticing that there were three cars in front, one of them belonging to my mother, I put the signal indicator on and turned into the driveway. Within seconds, three of my sisters, a couple of nieces and nephews and my mother came rushing out the door to greet us. As always, whether arriving or leaving, it was mandatory for everyone to cry, laugh and hug at the same time.

# Chapter 19
## The Treasure Hunt

The next morning, everyone was up early and raring to go. After a good old-fashioned breakfast of French toast (or "lost" bread as the French liked to call it) and bacon, I borrowed the house keys from my mother and started to leave with Francesca and Sonya.

"I think you're all crazy," were the last words she said as we headed out the door.

Since I could never resist having the last word, I shot back over my shoulder, "Yeah, well you know what they say about those who always follow the rules; they never make it into the history books!"

It took less than five minutes to get to the house, then another few minutes to unlatch the hatch that would lead us into the attic. It was a good thing we had thought of bringing flashlights along, or rather that my mother had reminded us to bring some.

Although spider webs covered the boxes we were supposed to be searching, for the next seven hours, with the exception of a quick break to eat takeout pizza, we put aside all arachnophobic thoughts and fished out anything remotely looking like a lead to a hooked rug. This included pouring over an endless litany of letters and papers filed randomly in boxes. Apparently some people in my family had been far less obsessive than I about dating their files.

Sonya found an old scribbler.

"Hey, look at this, girls. These look like ghost stories, judging by the illustrations. Have you read these before, Isabelle?"

"Let me see that." I was shocked that my father's old scribbler still existed. I thought it had been thrown away in one of my mother's manic housecleaning binges. Aside from the one hooked rug that he'd left me, I had nothing left of his artistry.

"Well? Are they spooky? You could translate them and read them to us?" suggested Francesca, her eyes flashing in the semidarkness.

"This is unbelievable. Remember during the drive last night when I said that there were three things I used to really look forward to every Christmas? Well, I never got to the part about the coolest and my most favourite Christmas tradition."

"Let me guess, it has something to do with ghost stories?" said Sonya.

"You got it. This is a compilation of ghost stories my father used to tell us on New Year's Day. It starts in 1966, the year I was born."

"Is that when the tradition started?"

"No, my oldest sister Thérèse had already left home and was working in the Northwest Territories by the time I was born. She came home that Christmas and suggested we start keeping a record of the stories. So the handwriting is mostly hers and the illustrations are my father's."

"Why New Year's Day? Is that an Acadian tradition?"

"Oh, no, though the Acadians are well-versed in ghost stories it was a tradition that started and ended with my father. Every New Year's Day we would start the day by taking the tree decorations down. Naturally that was depressing for us, but Papape found a way of making it just as exciting as the rest of the holiday. As soon as the decorations were all neatly packed away and ready for the next season, he would haul the tree to the basement and light the wood stove. Then the whole family would gather around the stove roasting marshmallows to the smell of burning pine while Papa spun his annual ghostly tale."

"That's a cool tradition. I think I might steal that one as soon as Poppy is old enough. I'm not all that great at reading aloud, but you are, Isabelle. You should continue this legacy of your father's by starting it up again in our family of friends." Then, as if it were an afterthought, she added, "That is, if you plan on coming back from Paris ..."

"That was sneaky even for you, Francesca. Of course, I'm coming back!"

"But what if that tarot reading comes true and you find your soulmate in Paris?"

"Hey, I didn't think you believed in all that stuff? Besides, he wouldn't be my soulmate if he didn't want to live in Nova Scotia."

Just then Sonya produced two books. It was a good thing, because Francesca and I were about to start crying again.

"Hey, look what I just found. Oh! I wonder what juicy stuff is in here? Fran, they're Isabelle's old journals."

"Sorry to disappoint, girls, but those aren't mine. Look at the dates. They belong to my grandmother. I'm sure I've told you before that I was named after her."

After seven hours, those were the only items we found that were of major interest, the ghost stories and my grandmother's two old journals. We were starting to get hungry again.

"You know what, I think if there was anything here that connects that hooked rug to anything, it's either gone or it's in this journal. I for one vote to go home to clean up before I start spinning my own webs. I swear I have spiders everywhere including my underwear."

I had a feeling all along that I wouldn't find anything up there. Something told me that this Garden of the Gods that the woman in my dream had told me about was the place where I'd find the clue that I needed. So far I hadn't found anything about the name except for its connection to the word Acadia."

Cold and hungry, we adjourned.

With the exception of one afternoon at the tavern, where I got to listen to my favourite Cape Breton fiddler, Ashley MacIsaac, I spent the rest of the holiday bonding with the family and especially with my mother.

I had managed to live up to my father's reputation. I was happy that on the eve of my departure to another land I was leaving behind a sentimental journey for my mother to enjoy all year. I had made the calendar myself. For each month, a photograph celebrated a memorable occasion in the family. Mére took the calendar out and proudly showed it to each visitor we received over the holiday season.

"Isn't she just like her father?" she would ask of each guest. For one of the first times since his passing, she wasn't referring to the stubbornness, pride, temper or any of the other less than wonderful *Piquine* traits that my father and I also shared.

Chéticamp — December 26, 2000

*Chère* Terry,

Wasn't sure if I'd have the chance to email you again before leaving but here I am. There was so much craziness with my packing, early Xmas parties and all. I just arrived at my sister's in Chéticamp for supper and realized that they have email access so that's how I am writing to you now.

Thank God, Tony decided not to move out when I told him about Paris. Otherwise I was going to impale myself on the nearest sharp object. Anything to avoid dealing with furniture storage.

Did I tell you that I went to see the rug lady. She thinks the rug is over two hundred years old. Can you imagine? Francesca and Sonya joined me for the first part of my stay in Chéticamp and helped me hunt for clues in the old family attic. Sadly, it was more like looking for a needle in a haystack (or hen's teeth as we say here). We found neither teeth nor needles.

I should get back to my family. Hope you're enjoying your Xmas. I'll call from the plane to confirm my arrival time. Don't worry if you can't meet me, I have the address, so I'll find you.

Manouche

# Chapter 20
## French Kiss

Sitting on the tarmac while the ground crew repaired a faulty engine didn't exactly seem like a good sign. Still, my gut wasn't saying that I absolutely needed to get off the plane. All my life, I had promised myself that if I were to sense something really ominous in an airplane, I would disembark immediately, even if that meant losing my airfare.

Almost an hour later than scheduled, the ground crew gave the thumbs up and the pilot got clearance to prepare for takeoff. Less than fifteen minutes later, we were flying over Halifax. From my window seat, I cast my eyes down at the city. This was the place where I had become confident, seeing my entire life ahead of me instead of lost somewhere and impossible to reach.

I felt so hyper-alive that during the flight I could hardly contain Neurotica's unhinged phobia. It would be such a pity to die now, full of dreams and anticipation of the days ahead. I glanced at the man sitting next to me and banished Neurotica to her chambers.

I took a deep breath and tried to relax. For thirty seconds or so I felt great. I checked my pockets for the familiar package of Pop Rocks. Crossing my legs very slowly, I turned to my neighbour and asked, "Have you ever tried kissing anyone with Pop Rocks in your mouth?"

He tried to smile, but looked as if he thought I was crazy.

When we were somewhere over the Atlantic, I reached into my carry-on bag and pulled out the small painting that Gilles and Sonya had given me at the airport. Since my seat neighbour hadn't turned out to be as scintillating as I'd hoped, I decided to become aloof instead.

Against a vibrant sunset with all the shades of red imaginable a lacy black bra stood out starkly on a thin clothesline just as I had imagined it would look in the photograph I'd tried to capture. The church steeple was also there, less prominent than in real life, with an ethereal or impressionistic quality as if it could fly away with the slightest breeze.

I wondered which paint strokes were Gilles' and which were Sonya's. I couldn't remember ever seeing a joint painting before except for church frescoes. As I held it in my hands, I felt the love these two friends shared. They would make an awesome married couple. I could hardly believe that it would be happening in less than two months. Gilles had proposed at Christmas. By the time they had dropped me off at the airport, they were both almost bursting at the seams with their next announcement.

They decided that they would fly to Paris and get married on St. Valentine's Day. And, they wanted me to be their maid of honour (or maid with no honour, whichever you prefer) since I had introduced them. Would I? Was there any question? Of course, I'd do it!

That was when they had produced the painting that was meant to be a witness thank you gift but that they couldn't bear to see me leave without. It lifted my spirits immensely knowing that we would all be together in just six weeks.

After replacing the painting in my carry-on bag, I pulled out the second of my grandmother's journals. I had skimmed both of them briefly over the holidays and, finding nothing about rugs, had decided to read them both cover to cover and relish the memories of Mémére Bella.

I had read up to December 31st, 1970 and had found lots of interesting tidbits about my own childhood as well as my father's.

1970 was around the time my grandparents moved in with us because Pépére had broken his hip. A funny part described Pépére's frustration when he tried building card houses in our household. Just when he would reach the end of the deck, invariably one of the grandkids or one of the many visitors would walk in and cause a puff of air that would knock over his little card castle.

Mémére Bella was either very practical in her entries, detailing weather forecasts and food deliveries, or she wrote with great imagination. One of my favourite entries was titled "… And then, the mosquitoes came …"

The entry that followed was a creative re-enactment of a camping trip we'd taken in Cape Breton Highlands National Park. By her observation of every type of insect that punctuated our activities, Mémére Bella was no great fan of bugs.

In this same entry, she described my first fishing trip with my father, the one everyone remembered because he planted the largest fish from his basket onto my fishing line. What! I cringed when I thought of how I had boasted to everyone that I'd caught the biggest fish. Whether it was true or not, he was always trying to convince us that either we were the best at everything, or that we were capable of becoming the best. No wonder we became so fiercely competitive.

This entry was followed by a furious rant about how back in 1936 the English government had expropriated a portion of land belonging to Acadian families for this National Park. She referred to "*le Cap Rouge*" and "*la Rigouèche*" as yet more proof that those "*maudits Anglais*" would stop at nothing to ensure that Acadians not prosper in this country.

Ah, but Mémére Bella would get her revenge yet. She went on to vow that she would demand in her will that all of her property be kept within the family and that if sold it had to be to Acadian descendents only. She kept her promise, too.

Now the only part of her vow that remained unfulfilled was a class action lawsuit that would have Acadians and especially those families displaced by the park compensated for their financial losses. Or as she had stated succinctly, "If only there was a good Acadian lawyer, we could sue the bastards."

Some time later I glanced at my sleeping neighbour's watch and noticed that we had less than half an hour or so before we started to descend. I figured this was as good a time as any to face what I'd been avoiding since takeoff. Reaching into my carry-on again, I pulled out the small package wrapped in the coolest monster paper *à la* Maurice Sendak's *Where the Wild Things Are*. It was from Tony.

I was surprised at the airport that Francesca had even agreed to deliver it for him. I had no idea what Tony had told her that morning, but Francesca was unusually gracious about her choice of words.

I unwrapped the small parcel quickly before losing my nerve. Inside was a single CD with a label on it in Tony's handwriting: "*Sonata para Isabella*". There was also a note:

Isabelle,

This is a piano sonata I composed for you. I love you. And I want you bad. The bitterness I've been wallowing in this past year is finally wearing off, I swear. I miss you terribly already. I want to hold you — maybe stroke you like a cat. I want to stroke you between your legs and make you love me. If you still want me, I'll be at home waiting for you.

And that is that.

Tony

"Excuse me, ladies and gentlemen, we will be starting our descent into Paris momentarily. In preparation for landing, we would ask all passengers at this time to ..."

I put Tony's CD away, and returned the food tray and my seat to their upright positions. Then I found myself praying to both my father and grandmother to assist the pilot in making a safe landing. When my neighbour noticed my tears, he turned compassionately and asked if I was flying for the first time. It was easier to tell him that it was than to try explaining my pathos.

It turns out, I was anxious needlessly. Although about forty-five minutes later than scheduled, touching down in Paris almost felt like a butterfly landing gracefully on a dewy leaf. Though it seemed like an eternity, it was actually only minutes before I stood inside the Charles de Gaulle airport scanning the crowd. I had just enough time to begin worrying again when I felt a tap on the shoulder and a bunch of sunflowers appeared before me.

"Isabelle?" The voice was masculine and hesitant.

I took a deep breath, pasted on my friendliest smile and turned around, trying my best to hide my disappointment.

"Hi, there! You must be Terry's brother. I recognize you from the photograph she sent me. She warned me that she might be held up at work, but I was secretly hoping that she might make it. Still, it's very sweet of you to come rescue me. I'm so sorry we're late. I told her that I could find my own way, but she insisted that ... well, you know."

I stopped just in time to remind myself of the impression I'd had of Gilles when I ran into him again in the fall. The last thing I wanted was for Terry's brother to think of me as frantic or neurotic. He was, after all, even more attractive than the photo I had seen of him with Terry. And, after that note from Tony it might not be a bad idea to try to find a diversion so I didn't go completely crazy. I took a second deep breath and held out my hand.

"Thanks so much for coming to meet me."

He surprised me then by taking my hand, lifting it slightly and placing a kiss on my palm, never once taking his eyes away from mine.

"Welcome to Paris, Isabelle." Handsome and charming.

Finally the sound of the luggage belt churning broke the spell and I disengaged myself as politely and casually as possible to go find my bags.

"Here, allow me. Where are your other bags?" He seemed concerned. I wondered if he was irritated at the possibility of having to stick around to locate lost luggage.

I told him that I had sent most of my belongings through the post so that I wouldn't have to lug them with me from the airport in case I had to find my way around the city alone. "The rest should arrive any day."

"Good thinking. Well, shall we?"

Terry's brother had lost his smile and now seemed consumed with worry about something other than luggage. As I followed the lines of his furrowed brow, I tried to trace the source of his anxiety. This delay may have been terribly inconvenient for him, on New

Year's Eve especially, and with this thought I created some furrows of my own. Of course, there was no point in asking since he wouldn't likely admit it to me. The best course of action was probably to keep quiet and let him manoeuvre us out of the airport and into the city as quickly as possible.

Moments later, I found myself squashed into a tiny French car and invigorated by the speed with which we were careening through traffic. It obviously hadn't taken Terry's brother very long to adapt to Parisian driving standards. Then again, if memory served me well, Montrealers had a similar *empressement*. In my breathless attempt to absorb all that was around me, I hardly even had the chance to get nervous about meeting Terry until the car jolted to a stop and my companion said his first words since departing the airport.

"Well, here we are!" He tried to make them sound enthusiastic, but for some reason his words sounded more like a death sentence.

As I climbed out of the car, I remembered that day long ago when Caroline and I had left Chéticamp. I hesitated a moment before asking, but decided this was something I really wanted.

"I'm sorry to bother you, but would you mind taking a quick photo of me in front of that sign. It's sort of one of my quirky traditions of tracing my departures and arrivals." I offered him my camera.

"Of course."

Just then an older woman came rushing out from the café across the street.

*"Attendez, pas si vite, obligez une vielle demoiselle. La photo sera sans doute plus jolie avec les deux, n'est-ce pas?"*

Terry's brother hesitated but I assured him that I was happy to have him in the photo. He stood next to me awkwardly. He seemed to have lost all of his earlier charm.

*"Allons-y, un baiser. Nous sommes à Montmartre et non pas la Bastille."*

A kiss! Good God, the old woman had mistaken us for a couple. I was about to correct her when I felt a hand behind my neck. Terry's brother was turning me towards him and now his face was approaching mine. Click.

My thoughts were racing madly at first but then I couldn't think any more. This was complete madness. This stranger was kissing me, alternating between amazing tenderness and fiery passion. And to make things even crazier I found myself responding with almost equal intensity. I might have even fantasized for a second that they were Tony's lips and not a complete stranger's. Was this what Paris did to people? No wonder it was called a city for lovers. Click. Click. Click-click. Where were those godamned Pop Rocks when you needed them?

The kiss ended. I took a step back and almost tripped over the sunflowers. When I turned to face him again, he reminded me of someone with serious gas pains.

"Hey, don't take it so hard. No harm done. It wasn't that bad. In fact, you're a pretty darn good kisser. Next time, you should just give a lady a little warning, that's all."

My attempt at humour fell flat. Terry's brother never even responded. He simply picked up the sunflowers and my suitcase and headed across the street to the café where that woman had come from.

Since I had very few options at that point, I decided to follow him. I watched him with curiosity. First he placed my suitcase down at a very secluded table in the corner. Then he walked up to the bar as if he owned the place and said something to the woman from before. Apparently she worked there. Then he signalled for me to join him at the table. Well, this was all getting a little too outrageous even for jet-lagged me.

"Actually, if it's all the same to you, I would just as soon wait for …"

But he cut me off.

"Please just sit down. I have a note for you to read." As he spoke the words, he pulled an envelope from his shirt pocket and handed it to me. "It's from Terry."

I sat down and opened the envelope:

*Chère* Isabelle,

This is the hardest letter I have ever had to write …

I paused and glanced at his pained expression across the table. The woman from behind the bar came along then and placed two cups of coffee and shots of what looked like cognac. They were at least doubles. Before leaving, the woman gave me a sympathetic look, squeezed my hand and said, *"Soyez gentil, il est vraiment pas un mauvais gars."*

Be gentle. What the hell? Was jet lag making me delirious? I poured some cream into my coffee, stirred it nervously and took a big swig of the alcohol before continuing with the letter. Yes, it was cognac, Remy Martin, my favourite.

Where to start? It began as a typo but in the end, it was a deception. I have deceived you and I don't know how to apologize. I wish I could tell you myself but I have a feeling you would never let me finish. I wish I had said something before you got on that plane. I even tried to page you at the airport, but you didn't answer.

Remember a long time ago when I wrote to you with a confession and told you that I was a GAY? Well, that was supposed to be spelled GUY …

I looked up and saw the pained expression across the table for what it was. Only then did it finally sink in that the eyes looking at me were not Terry's brother's.

All the ominous sensations and weird vibrations hadn't been my imagination at all. Now all of those sensations exploded inside me in a white rage only someone who knows a *Piquine* could imagine. I could feel the blood draining from my face and my grip on the letter tightened into a fist. I wasn't even sure what would come out, since there were so many insults that sprang to mind. In the end, I didn't scream or rant or rave. My voice dry and quiet and dripping with disgust simply demanded that he leave me alone immediately.

It was impossible to see through this blind rage, so I never even noticed him getting up and leaving. I just kept staring at the ball of paper in my hands and tried to will my heartbeat to return to normal.

— *Poor guy, I suppose that typo was your doing, said the son. Have you no pity?*

*— Certainly it was my doing, said Bella, I didn't have infinite means of directing Isabelle to her destiny.*

*— But look at him, Mother, he seems broken.*

*— My son, pity is a human feeling. Besides, a broken heart can make him stronger. He'll have to dig deep which is not such a bad thing.*

*— And what about Isabelle? She's had more than her share, don't you think?*

*— Have faith in the little one. She's about to discover why she's in Paris.*

*— You are in charge as usual, Mother. Please go on.*


When I did finally look up again, he was gone and the woman from the bar was sitting across from me. She waited for a minute or so, perhaps in case I decided to say anything. I gave her a blank stare that might have lasted forever had she not placed a set of keys on the table and pushed them towards me. She then informed me that the room at the top of the stairs was mine for as long as I needed it. It included breakfast, there was no charge and no one would bother me.

As angry as I was, my survival instincts were kicking in and I knew this was too good a deal to pass up. I was about to take the keys when a thought made me hesitate. As if she could read my mind, the woman said.

*"Non, il n'a pas payé la chambre. Je le considère le garçon que j'n'ai jamais eu. Je suis vielle assez pour me rendre compte que tu n'accepterais jamais sa générosité, mais pourquoi pas celle d'une veuve solitaire?"*

No, he hadn't paid for the room. This woman considered him to be the son she'd never had and so why deny an old widow like her one of the few things she could do for someone? I considered this for a moment. The woman picked up the keys, placed them in my hand and closed her hand over mine.

*"Je m'appelles Sandrine, si tu as besoin de quelque chose ..."*

With those words, Sandrine got up and went back behind the bar.

I got up stiffly, took my suitcase and began to climb up the back staircase that led to my new Parisian home. I paused and looked back over my shoulder. Sandrine went back over to the table where I had left the sunflowers behind on purpose. She picked them up and went back behind the bar to put them in a vase. As she poured water into the vase, her tears plopped inside like raindrops.

# Chapter 21
## Voices from the Past

The next thing I remembered hearing was a knock on the door. I must have fallen asleep. I wrapped the blanket I'd slept in around me and kangarooed to the door like a jumping bean racing across hot coals, except in this case the coals were more like ice cubes. Seeing no one through the peephole, I opened the door. There was a breakfast tray and a note from Sandrine:

*J'ai pensé que tu voudrais prendre le déjeuner seul.*
— Sandrine

I took the tray and carried it to the small balcony just off my room. I was grateful that it faced a small courtyard rather than the side of the street where Terry supposedly lived. It was cold, but I didn't care. I also realized that this privacy would be short-lived if I decided to stay for any length of time. It was only a matter of time before Terry and I would run into each other if we lived on the same street.

Damn him all to hell. I had more practical matters to resolve. First things first. I had to call my mother and Francesca to let them know I'd made it safe and sound, and that I could be reached at another number.

What would I tell them, though? Obviously, I couldn't say anything to my mother just yet or she would worry herself into an early grave. Francesca on the other hand would undoubtedly press for details. At least Tony had kept the apartment, so I didn't have to worry about that.

The solution was obvious. I would simply regard this as an unplanned vacation, forget about Terry and make the best of it. At least I didn't have to pay for my room. What's that great line? "When your big ship sinks, get in your little boat and row."

I walked back into the room, picked up the phone and dialed the café number. Sandrine picked up.

*"Oui?"*

I thanked her for the breakfast and asked about making an overseas call. Sandrine said she was giving me an outside line and that we could make billing arrangements later. Before I could even say thank you, the line clicked and the dial tone came on.

I began dialling my mother's number. It would be just after lunchtime in Canada. She picked up on the second ring.

*"Bonne et Heureuse Année!"* Happy New Year. Holy shit. I had slept right through New Year's Eve. There must have been fireworks and all other kinds of noisemakers.

My mother was so happy to hear from me, it made me want to cry. She told me about watching the New Year's celebrations on television and looking for me in the crowds of Paris. She said she was sure she got a glimpse of me. I didn't bother correcting her.

All in all, it was a great phone call. I even broached the subject of coming back earlier than I'd anticipated saying that the translating job looked easier than I had expected. Two months max. This, of course, delighted her.

With the first hurdle over, I decided to save the call to Francesca for later. Instead, I would get dressed, pack a small backpack and explore a corner of Paris I didn't know very well.

I walked for hours. When I finally couldn't stand my aching feet any longer, I made my way towards the Eiffel Tower. Once there I sat on a bench and read my grandmother's entry for New Year's Day, 1971:

Well, it's been a day for throwing out the old and bringing in the new. So, after the annual ghost story, I set out to do as much throwing out as possible (bearing in mind the spirit of my eccentric great-grandmother Patronille, an enthusiastic collector herself who was forced to leave so many of her belongings behind in Paris). This next move will be the most difficult one for me. At least the one to the coffin will have to be done by someone else.

Yes, sir, my son has decided to move to a bigger house down the street. He must have lost his head thinking we'll all live to be a hundred. I think he and little Bella have both inherited this eccentricity. I wonder if Bella will remember the legacy I am trying to pass on when she's all grown up. The only words I have to remember Patronille by — eccentricity, she swore in the note, was a sharpened awareness of life's ineffable secrets.

Even at my age,
There's an adventurous spirit in me,
A spirit that craves the thrill of moving
Maybe in circles unknown.

It is perhaps the predestined pull
Of the tides that move within;
At least this voyage shall leave behind
An especially genuine treasure,
One I sincerely hope little Bella
Will return to reclaim.

She will survive; she will be strong,
Stronger than she thinks.
She inspires me to believe in the future.
I will bring a little of her sparkle with me
And leave my own little gem for her discovery.
She will be the inheritor of our collective wisdom.

Bella, January 1st, 1971

— *It's about time she heard my name, Patronille said.*
— *Yes Mother, couldn't we have fast-forwarded to this before?*
— *My son, patience was never your strong suit in life and neither is it in no time. I hope Isabelle will be learning this lesson sooner rather than later. Now will you let me finish?*

## Chapter 22
### *Jardin des Dieux*

The room above the café was as bleak as I had left it the week before. I had been away in Germany during that time. On New Year's Day, I found out that the archives wouldn't open for a week. I had decided that the only way to completely avoid Terry was to get the hell out of Paris. And so, I did something I'd been wanting to do my whole life. I walked into a train station, went straight to the ticket counter and bought a ticket on the very next train that was leaving. When the ticket agent forced me to pick a stop, I decided on Stuttgart for no particular reason.

I had just started unpacking when I found another note from Sandrine, this time apologizing for the lack of heat. It seemed some municipal department had to turn it on and they were on an extended Christmas holiday until the Monday following New Year's. This meant at least one more night of bitter cold. At least I had a small two-burner stove. Sandrine had also left a can of hot chocolate, an electric blanket, some candles and a pile of flyers on the side table.

Once the candles were lit and the hot chocolate was made, I wrapped myself in as many blankets as I could find, as well as the electric one. It was quite cozy. I opened the paper bag I'd brought back that contained a *Croque Monsieur*, a fancy French name for a greasy sandwich, and reached into my purse for Mémére Bella's journal. In that first week of the new millennium, I must have read that entry about a thousand times and I was still reeling from it.

I had never even heard about an ancestor named Patronille. Furthermore, I still remembered that dullard of a history teacher who crushed my one and only foray into the lives of my female ancestors. I'd had the idea for a project that would uncover the lives of pioneering French women who'd left France, crossed the Atlantic and survived both the harsh Canadian landscape and the lack of amenities they were used to back in *la mère patrie*. The dullard had informed me that I would have to find another topic because I would never find anything of value about the wives of the *Quatorze Vieux*, the fourteen men who had supposedly founded Chéticamp on their own.

I couldn't wait for the archives in Paris to reopen so I could find out if Patronille had been registered anywhere. Two more days. With every passing day I was feeling more confident that Patronille was part of the key to finding out the exact origins of my hooked rug. After all, what other treasure could my grandmother have been referring to? In any event, we had scoured the entire attic during our treasure hunt over the holidays. If there had been any other treasure, I was certain we would have found it.

There was nothing to do but wait and I was never very good at that. At least the trip to Germany had distracted me. The weather had even been good enough to rent a bicycle. On the last day before returning to Paris I went cycling through dead cornfields. I found a most enchanting tree house tucked away, climbed into it and finished reading the rest of Mémére's journals. On the way back, I spotted an interesting piece of graffiti written (in English!) on a tree. It said:

The only age
Some people respect
Is in a wine bottle

Back in my frosty room, I heard a sweet rhapsody coming from outside. It sounded like all the birds of Paris were practising for a concerto. No matter how hard I tried, it was impossible in a city renowned for its lovers not to think of Tony and the sonata he'd composed for me. Nor could I completely forget about Terry and that malapropos kiss.

As sleepiness came over me, I wondered if I'd ever understand why the cruel wind of deception had destroyed our friendship. In one fell swoop, it had swept away all the leaves from a passion tree in bud, leaving a desolate skeleton.

On a normal day Neurotica would have accused me of being too naive, but Paris wasn't an easy place for her to control me. And Erotica had been mute since my arrival.

•　　•　　•

I couldn't remember whether I slept much that next night, but when the sun finally began to thaw my little igloo, I was already awake and grateful that the day promised warmth. I reached for the pile of flyers on the nightstand and noticed that on top of the pile was a card from the post office advising that there was a parcel for me to pick up. That would be the bags I'd sent ahead from Canada, when I thought I'd be in Paris for longer than two weeks. I wondered, if they were never claimed, whether they would be returned to sender. At least that would save the price of shipping them a second time.

The rest of the flyers were mostly advertising, either restaurants in the area or the extension of post-Christmas sales into the New Year. I was about to put them all back when I noticed one flyer in a deep crimson shade with big black bold letters that read, *Inauguration du Jardin des Dieux*.

I did a double take when I realized that this was the name of the place the woman in my dream had told me to return to: Garden of the Gods. Obviously, this couldn't be the place she'd meant if this was a grand opening. After all, I couldn't return to a place that hadn't existed before, could I? And yet, I was curious enough that I made a mental note of the address and that the opening would be at 2:00 PM. that very afternoon. I then proceeded to enjoy my hot chocolate and sandwich.

Around 2:00 PM., I was in the neighbourhood of the *Jardins des Dieux*, so I thought I might as well pop in to see whether I recognized any of the surroundings. The address was for a large park that I remembered well. The Garden of the Gods must have been the name of a small section of the park that was being rededicated to someone or something. I decided to take a stroll and explore the grounds a bit.

I had been walking for about twenty minutes and hadn't seen or heard any signs of an inauguration when I noticed a statue of a soldier just ahead and decided to find out who the French were honouring these days. It came as quite a surprise to discover that the soldier was a woman. And not just any woman, but an evocative figure that stirred the edges of my recollection.

I spotted a small plaque at the base of the statue and went over to read it. The words were so shocking that I had to sit down on the grass. I'd been staring at them for god knows how long when someone came up and startled me from behind.

"Excuse me, *Mademoiselle*, forgive my intrusion. You seem captivated by this statue, but you will catch your death if you stay on that cold grass very long."

I simply looked up, smiled and didn't move.

"I work for park heritage and this also happens to be one of my favourite statues. It has such *mystique, non?*"

"Do you know anything about her?"

"I certainly do, *Mademoiselle*. What in particular would you like to know?"

"I haven't really had a chance to think about it. I guess nothing in particular and everything in general or everything in particular and nothing in general?"

"Oh, Mademoiselle has a sense of humour, I see. Well, the silent heroine, Patronille Desveaux, is a bit of legend and one would gather from these legends that she also had a sense of humour."

"Really. How so?"

"Well, maybe a trickster is a better way of saying. They say that the silent heroine of the Revolution was originally from the coast of Normandy. Some have said St. Malo, but I don't think that was ever established. Anyway, legend has it that she escaped her small village when she heard about all the trouble here in Paris and came to help the Resistance."

"You say that this is from a legend. Are there any records that prove any of this?"

"Well, you know, *Mademoiselle*, the world is changing and there seems to be less and less to go around for that kind of historical research. It makes me very sad in my occupation. I mean, I'm sure there are some documents around, but it takes time and money to do that kind of detailed research."

"But you said you knew about her. What else do you know?"

"You are very curious, *Mademoiselle*. Let's see — well, I know that Mlle. Desveaux was an artist and that she used that as a cover for her role in organizing the mob of women that invaded the royal palace at Versailles in October of 1789. It has also been said that she was the confidant of Charlotte Corday, who stabbed Jean Paul Marat. There is even reason to suspect that Mlle. Desveaux and Mlle. Corday may have travelled to Paris together, since they were both from Normandy. It also seems that when she first arrived in Paris, our capricious heroine got a job at the same hat shop as Countess du Barry, who later became the mistress of King Louis XV. Now the Countess and Mlle. Corday were both guillotined, but Mlle. Desveaux somehow escaped. See, that's why I think she was a bit of a trickster."

"Wow! I do remember the names of Corday and Marat from art history class. There's a well-known painting from the Reign of Terror called "The Death of Marat" by Jacques Louis David that depicts the stabbing. But I can't remember, why was Countess du Barry guillotined?"

"The Countess was accused of aiding the so-called enemies of the state and there were rumblings that she was passing on information, quite likely to Patronille here, who'd remained friends with her since their work at the hat shop. It is even rumoured that the Countess managed to commission some kind of tapestries by her, as a cover you know, for entering the royal palace. However, since those have never been located, it's probably impossible to prove. Quite likely, even if they did exist they were burned during the fires."

Or not! My insides began feeling like a sky filled with fireworks.

"You are like an encyclopedia on this topic."

"Like I said before, I am a fan of this statue. It has a certain *je ne sais quoi* that appeals to my romantic side. Even when we get old, we still have to keep a little romance alive, no?"

"So what happened to Patronille after the Revolution? Where did she go?"

"Now, here is where it gets even more like legend and less factual. Of the few historians who have followed her life, most believe that she returned to Brittany, married and changed her first name at the time of the marriage so that no one would find her."

"Uh hmm. And, what do the others think?"

"Well, there is a small group, maybe two historians, who lean toward the more romantic notion that she hid on a boat as a stowaway and ended up in North America at the time that France was building new colonies there."

"Really? This is fascinating Mr. ...?"

"Oh, I'm sorry, I'm living up to the namesake of Paris by being so rude. My name is Guillonet, Sylvain Guillonet."

"I'm very pleased to have made your acquaintance Mr. Guillonet. My name is Isabelle. Isabelle Desveaux."

"You're not serious. Desveaux? Are you from the same line of Desveaux in Normandy?"

"Actually, Mr. Marat, I am an Acadian from Canada and I do know that my ancestors originated in Normandy, but it also so happens that my great-great-great-great-grandmother arrived on a boat that originated in Paris. And her name, I recently learned, was none other than Patronille Desveaux."

"*Mon Dieu, qu'est-ce que vous me dites?* I can hardly believe my ears. I have fantasized that this could happen some day, but who would've thought that it would be on this ordinary day in January? I am so honoured to meet you." Mr. Guillonet was getting down on his knees at this point.

"*Monsieur, monsieur*, please get up. Here, I will get up with you."

"Oh, *mon Dieu*, I don't know what to say now. I feel like a fool. You must have known all this before."

"No, no, you're wrong. I had never even laid eyes on this statue before today and I certainly didn't know any of this history that you've shared with me today, legend or not."

"Really? Then I have helped you perhaps in some way?"

"Mr. Guillonet, I think you may have just changed my entire life ..."

With those words, the tears that I had been storing since my first night in Paris began spilling out.

"Oh what can I do, *Mademoiselle*? You are so sad. Why are you so sad? This should be a happy day, no?"

"Yes I am happy, these are tears of happiness not sadness. I just can't believe all that I have learned, and just because of a flyer about *les Jardins des Dieux*?"

"Jardins des Dieux? What is that, *Mademoiselle*?"

"I got a pamphlet at my hotel that said there would be an inauguration for *Jardins des Dieux* here at 2:00 PM."

"That's impossible, *Mademoiselle*. I've been working here for over thirty years and I've never heard of such a place. *En plus*, this park is nearly deserted this time of year. I only come by once or twice a day ..."

"I'm telling you that I got this pamphlet in my hotel room in Montmartre that ..."

"I know what you say, but like I said this time of year, I only come here once or twice a day to try and keep the vagabond population down. I was coming by today because there's a man who's been showing up here around this time everyday for the last week. He carries a big birdhouse around with him and looks pretty down on his luck. I think he might be thinking of setting up in this area."

For the first time in almost an hour, there was a long silence. I kept staring at the statue, it was so hard to keep my eyes off it.

Finally, a woman with eyes and a face, features similar to mine, beautifully carved and having weathered centuries of silence. A head in the clouds and not in the sand. This felt like the greatest moment of my life. I only wished that Francesca and Sonya had been with me to share it. How I missed my friends!

"Oh, look, there's our gentleman now." Mr. Guillonet was pointing past the statue.

It seemed impossible that anything else could surprise me, but seeing Terry walking sullenly lugging a large red birdhouse was almost more than I could stand. I started laughing and couldn't stop. By the end, I was keeled over and holding my stomach. I was laughing so hard I was in pain.

"*Mademoiselle*, what is so funny? I don't think I understand Canadian humour."

"Oh, Monsieur Guillonet, you know the story of Patronille. Well, this is just as legendary and just as complicated. I can tell you one thing, this gentleman isn't a vagabond. He's just been waiting for me to show up, that's all."

Terry had heard me laughing, had stopped and was staring at me now. He was probably wondering what the hell was so funny.

For my part, I felt so exhausted from laughing that I wasn't even angry any more.

"Hey, Terry, come on over here and meet Monsieur Guillonet."

Terry headed over hesitantly. He stopped about five yards away.

"Look, Isabelle, you might think this is a bad idea, but, I really wanted to apologize, and I thought if I built you a birdhouse like your father built, you might believe I was sincere and ..."

"Oh, can it, Terry. You're much funnier when you're talking about axe murderers. I forgive you, okay? Actually, no, I don't forgive you, I'm just ready to move forward with my head in the clouds, like Patronille here."

"I ... I don't know what to say."

I reached into my pocket for the familiar package, tore it open and held it out to Terry.

"Don't say anything. Just shut up, take a handful of Pop Rocks and prepare for some fireworks."

# Epilogue

Somewhere over the Atlantic, February 16, 2001

Dear Francesca,

Hours away by plane, almost an ocean apart, I give you my latest supporting role.

*Dear Papape*, I thought, *help me do this without getting all sentimental.* Erotica and Neurotica graciously remained seated as I got up and walked up to the podium.

So let me tell you about the first birds to arrive at my birdhouse. I can't tell you about the very first bird, because he or she arrived with many others. They arrived as a family. In fact, they reminded me of all of you and especially of my two dear friends, Gilles and Sonya. Until I witnessed the love blossoming between these two, I'd convinced myself that true love was a thing of the past, a memory relegated to my parents and a bygone era.

But I was wrong. Love will never be old fashioned. And today we are all living proof of that as we gather here to celebrate that love.

I was thinking that my role called for some words of wisdom and that it would be fitting if I'd found something wise to say about that very important theme, love. But in the end, I decided that love most often comes upon us when we are truly alive. So instead, I have brought a poem about being alive to share with you. I guess it pretty much sums it up for me. It's a poem by Yeats.

"A Coat

"I made my song a coat
Covered with embroideries
Of old mythologies
From heel to throat
But the fools caught it
And wore it in the world's eyes
As though they'd wrought it
A song — let them take it
For there's more enterprise
In walking naked.

"Indeed, here's to walking naked, to baring our souls, to love, to madness, to creation and imagination! Let us endeavour as a family of friends to walk naked with each other.

"It is so very easy in our complicated world to be a beautiful heroine or a handsome hero in a tragic story. But I for one never want to be a sad character from fiction. We are all too young to live through someone else and will never grow old enough for that either. We are always the right age to allow ourselves to belong to one another and to discover that this is what makes us most human.

"Now I ask you to raise your glasses with me. In French we say *Levons nos verres*. So, *levons nos verres* to my two dear friends, Gilles and Sonya."

We drank and the heavens opened and the rain came gushing down. Quite likely tears of happiness from all the guardian angels looking on. And, in those few fateful moments, there was just enough time for the angels' tears to seep into me and bless a magical seed that was already sprouting with the passionate strides and spirit of a *Piquine* tiger.

Love,
Isabelle

    *— Whoa, hold on a minute, said the son. If this is my grandchild, I demand to know who the father is.*
    *— Can't help you my dear. That is Isabelle's story to tell, not mine.*
    *— Tell me then, is Isabelle never to find love?*

*— My son, haven't you been paying attention? Isabelle found her great love near the beginning of my story. The time wasn't right, that's all. And great loves do survive all time. Patience, I tell you, patience. Soon enough, she will be telling you herself.*
*— Listen you two, interrupted Patronille, stop haggling. Now the world knows that I existed, isn't that enough for one story?*

# Acknowledgements

Although the characters, situations, and relationships in this book are fictional, the narrative dealing with the region of Chéticamp and its history has been greatly informed by the work of those who came before me.

Of course, this book would have been impossible to write without the support provided by my family and circle of friends. In particular, Thérèse (Aucoin) Desveaux — Merci Mama pour ton amour, pour ta générosité, et pour ta patience. À mes soeurs, Bernice, Nora, Lucille, Isabelle et Imelda: Merci pour votre appui dans mes divers projets. Merci pour la générosité que vous avez hérité de nos parents. Bernice, tout en particulier, tu m'as inspiré avec ton courage. Margie (Davis) Vigneault — Thank you for always having an open door. Your tireless efforts in the pursuit of democratic ideals and affordable childcare inspire me. Cristina (Queralt) Rafales — muchísimas gracias por tu amistad, tu energía y por llevar a Benjamin en mi vida. Eres mi hermana de espíritu. Tanya (Roach) Holt — yhank you for helping me survive Chéticamp. I never could have done it without you. Stephanie Tarr — thank you for adding a little sanity into my days of rewrites, thanks for challenging the mainstream agenda with your analysis and for sharing your amazing stories. Susan (Morrison) Cook — thank you for the drama and for providing women with opportunities to gather and share their creativity. Heather Asbil — thank you for living so harmoniously with Mother Nature and ALL her creatures. Brenda Lozier — thank you for your courage and persistence in your battle to break free from the cycle of abuse, for trusting me with your journey and for sharing your history with me. Eva Burkle — thank you for your friendship and your belief in my capacity for sanity and for discovering my Scorpio rising which has allowed me to embrace rather than deny my fiery nature. Joy Matthews — thank you for your belief in fate and your unique ability to make me laugh. Tanja Krajcinovic — thank you for surviving a war and for sharing your experiences with me and especially, with the youth who came to Canada as refugees. You are an inspiration to them as you are to me. Mamie Fraser — thank you for sharing your memories of Lillian Burke. Last but not least, I owe a mountain of gratitude to some men who provided me with their love, inspiration, contributions and/or support: André Narbonne, Hal Brinton, Joe Blades, Firdaus Bhathena, Simon Vigneault, Batra Calamari, Dan Callis, Richard Cumyn, and finally to my father, James Laurent Desveaux who from some other place continues to believe in me and give me the confidence to do anything I set my mind to.

# A Selection of Our Titles in Print

*A Fredericton Alphabet* (John Leroux) photos, architecture, ISBN 1-896647-77-4
*All the Perfect Disguises* (Lorri Neilsen Glenn) poetry, 1-55391-010-9
*Antimatter* (Hugh Hazelton) poetry, 1-896647-98-7
*Avoidance Tactics* (Sky Gilbert) drama, 1-896647-50-2
*Bathory* (Moynan King) drama, 1-896647-36-7
*Break the Silence* (Denise DeMoura) poetry, 1-896647-87-1
*Combustible Light* (Matt Santateresa) poetry, 0-921411-97-9
*Crossroads Cant* (Mary Elizabeth Grace, Mark Seabrook, Shafiq, Ann Shin. Joe Blades, editor)
     poetry, 0-921411-48-0
*Cuerpo amado/ Beloved Body* (Nela Rio; Hugh Hazelton, translator) poetry, 1-896647-81-2
*Day of the Dog-tooth Violets* (Christina Kilbourne) fiction, 1-896647-44-8
*During Nights That Undress Other Nights/ En las noches que desvisten otras noches* (Nela Rio;
     Elizabeth Gamble Miller, translator) poetry, 1-55391-008-7
*Garden of the Gods* (Dina Desveaux) novel, 1-55391-018-4
*Great Lakes logia* (Joe Blades, editor) art & writing anthology, 1-896647-70-7
*Heaven of Small Moments* (Allan Cooper) poetry, 0-921411-79-0
*Herbarium of Souls* (Vladimir Tasic) short fiction, 0-921411-72-3
*Jive Talk: George Fetherling in Interviews and Documents* (Joe Blades, editor), 1-896647-54-5
*Mangoes on the Maple Tree* (Uma Parameswaran) novel, 1-896647-79-0
*Manitoba highway map* (rob mclennan) poetry, 0-921411-89-8
*Memories of Sandy Point, St' George's Bay, Newfoundland* (Phyllis Pieroway), memoir, local history,
     1-55391--029-X
*Paper Hotel* (rob mclennan) poetry, 1-55391-004-4
*Railway Station* (karl wendt) poetry, 0-921411-82-0
*Reader Be Thou Also Ready* (Robert James) fiction, 1-896647-26-X
*resume drowning* (Jon Paul Fiorentino) poetry, 1-896647-94-4
*Shadowy:Technicians: New Ottawa Poets* (rob mclennan, editor), poetry, 0-921411-71-5
*Singapore* (John Palmer) drama, 1-896647-85-5
*Song of the Vulgar Starling* (Eric Miller) poetry, 0-921411-93-6
*Speaking Through Jagged Rock* (Connie Fife) poetry, 0-921411-99-5
*Starting from Promise* (Lorne Dufour) poetry, 1-896647-52-9
*Sunset* (Pablo Urbanyi; Hugh Hazelton, translator) novel, 1-55391-014-1
*Sustaining the Gaze/Sosteniendo la mirada/Soutenant le regard* (Brian Atkinson, Nela Rio, Elizabeth
     Gamble Miller & Jill Valéry (translators)), photographs, poetry, 1-55391-028-1
*Sweet Mother Prophesy* (Andrew Titus) fiction, 1-55391-002-8
*Tales for an Urban Sky* (Alice Major) poetry, 1-896647-11-1
*The Longest Winter* (Julie Doiron, Ian Roy) photos, short fiction, 0-921411-95-2
*This Day Full of Promise* (Michael Dennis) poetry, 1-896647-48-0
*The Sweet Smell of Mother's Milk-Wet Bodice* (Uma Parameswaran) fiction, 1-896647-72-3
*The Yoko Ono Project* (Jean Yoon) drama, 1-55391-001-X
*Túnel de proa verde/Tunnel of the Green Prow* (Nela Rio; Hugh Hazelton, translator) poetry,
     1-896647-10-3
*What Was Always Hers* (Uma Parameswaran) short fiction, 1-896647-12-X

**www.brokenjaw.com** hosts our current catalogue, submissions guidelines, manuscript award competitions, trade sales representation and distribution information. Directly from us, all individual orders must be prepaid. Please add $2.50 shipping per book. All Canadian orders must add 7% GST/HST (CCRA number: 892667403RT0001).

BROKEN JAW PRESS Inc.
Box 596 Stn A
Fredericton NB E3B 5A6
Canada